Holiday Hostage
A Zoe Donovan Mystery

by

Kathi Daley

I want to thank the very talented Jessica Fischer for the cover art.

I so appreciate Bruce Curran, who is always ready and willing to answer my cyber questions; Jayme Maness for helping out with the book clubs; and Peggy Hyndman for helping sleuth out those pesky typos.

And, of course, thanks to the readers and bloggers in my life, who make doing what I do possible.

Thank you to Randy Ladenheim-Gil for the editing.

And finally, I want to thank my husband Ken for allowing me time to write by taking care of everything else.

Books by Kathi Daley
Come for the murder, stay for the romance

Zoe Donovan Cozy Mystery:
Halloween Hijinks
The Trouble With Turkeys
Christmas Crazy
Cupid's Curse
Big Bunny Bump-off
Beach Blanket Barbie
Maui Madness
Derby Divas
Haunted Hamlet
Turkeys, Tuxes, and Tabbies
Christmas Cozy
Alaskan Alliance
Matrimony Meltdown
Soul Surrender
Heavenly Honeymoon
Hopscotch Homicide
Ghostly Graveyard
Santa Sleuth
Shamrock Shenanigans
Kitten Kaboodle
Costume Catastrophe
Candy Cane Caper
Holiday Hangover
Easter Escapade
Camp Carter
Trick or Treason
Reindeer Roundup
Hippity Hoppity Homicide

Firework Fiasco
Henderson House
Holiday Hostage
Lunacy Lake – *Summer 2019*

Zimmerman Academy The New Normal
Zimmerman Academy New Beginnings
Ashton Falls Cozy Cookbook

Tj Jensen Paradise Lake Mysteries by Henery Press:

Pumpkins in Paradise
Snowmen in Paradise
Bikinis in Paradise
Christmas in Paradise
Puppies in Paradise
Halloween in Paradise
Treasure in Paradise
Fireworks in Paradise
Beaches in Paradise
Thanksgiving in Paradise – *Fall 2019*

Whales and Tails Cozy Mystery:

Romeow and Juliet
The Mad Catter
Grimm's Furry Tail
Much Ado About Felines
Legend of Tabby Hollow
Cat of Christmas Past
A Tale of Two Tabbies
The Great Catsby
Count Catula
The Cat of Christmas Present

A Winter's Tail
The Taming of the Tabby
Frankencat
The Cat of Christmas Future
Farewell to Felines
A Whisker in Time
The Catsgiving Feast
A Whale of a Tail – *Spring 2019*

Writers' Retreat Southern Seashore Mystery:

First Case
Second Look
Third Strike
Fourth Victim
Fifth Night
Sixth Cabin
Seventh Chapter
Eighth Witness – *January 2019*

Rescue Alaska Paranormal Mystery:

Finding Justice
Finding Answers
Finding Courage
Finding Christmas
Finding Motive – *Spring 2019*

A Tess and Tilly Mystery:
The Christmas Letter
The Valentine Mystery
The Mother's Day Mishap
The Halloween House
The Thanksgiving Trip
The Saint Paddy's Promise – *March 2019*

The Inn at Holiday Bay:
Boxes in the Basement
Letters in the Library – *February 2019*
Message in the Mantle – *Spring 2019*

Family Ties:
The Hathaway Sisters
Harper – *Spring 2019*
Harlow – *Summer 2019*
Haven – *Fall 2019*
Haley – *Winter 2019*

Haunting by the Sea:
Homecoming by the Sea
Secrets by the Sea
Missing by the Sea
Deception by the Sea – *Spring 2019*
Betrayal by the Sea – *Summer 2019*
Christmas by the Sea – *Fall 2019*

Sand and Sea Hawaiian Mystery:
Murder at Dolphin Bay
Murder at Sunrise Beach
Murder at the Witching Hour

Murder at Christmas
Murder at Turtle Cove
Murder at Water's Edge
Murder at Midnight

Seacliff High Mystery:
The Secret
The Curse
The Relic
The Conspiracy
The Grudge
The Shadow
The Haunting

Road to Christmas Romance:
Road to Christmas Past

Chapter 1

Saturday, December 15

"Please state your name for the record," said the fed who'd identified himself as Agent Stanwell. He wore a white dress shirt, a black tie, and a black suit, which screamed authority, but I still wasn't sure which branch of the federal government he worked for. My best guess was FBI, although I couldn't quite figure out why an agent of the FBI would ask me to meet him in the suite of his hotel rather than the sheriff's office where I imagined Sheriff Salinger was working on the same murder case he was.

"Zoe Donovan Zimmerman," I answered in a strong voice as Agent Stanwell turned on the small tape recorder he'd set on the table between us.

"Do you know why I asked you to meet me here, Ms. Zimmerman?"

I looked around the room, which featured a large sitting area decorated for the holiday. It was cozy, with a sofa, two chairs, and a nice fireplace, but it still didn't seem fitting for this interview. "I guess it must have to do with what happened at Zarek Woodson's party last night."

"Please state for the record why you were in attendance at the party."

I glanced out the window at the falling snow and then back at the man sitting across from my position on the sofa. "Zarek held a cocktail party to introduce Senator Goodman to the men and women in the community whose support he hoped to garner. As you probably know, Goodman intends to run for governor as a step, I believe, to eventually making a run for the presidency. According to Zarek, Goodman wanted the chance to schmooze the people with the financial means to help him in his effort."

"And do you and your husband support Senator Goodman in his campaign to run for governor?"

I narrowed my gaze. "Actually, no. Zak and I don't support the senator or his politics. Is that relevant?"

He lifted a brow. "So you attended a meet and greet for a man whose politics you don't support?"

"Zarek is a friend of sorts who asked us to attend the party, so we did, although we planned to simply make an appearance and leave early."

"I see." The agent's tone indicated he didn't see at all.

I couldn't quite quell the need to defend our actions, even though I wasn't on trial here. Was I? "Looking back, maybe attending a party to introduce a politician we don't support may seem odd, but Zarek lives in Ashton Falls, and because he hired Zak's company to totally revamp the computer system for the ski resort he worked for until recently, the two knew each other. I guess you could even say they were friends. Zarek convinced Zak that just stopping by the party would really help him out, so eventually Zak agreed."

"Would you say Mr. Woodson supported Senator Goodman's political agenda?"

"I have no idea if Zarek supported the senator or even what Zarek's political orientation might have been. What I do know is that Zarek needed the senator. You see, he wanted to build a luxury ski resort near Ashton Falls. An elite resort that would cater to the very rich. He'd hit some snags getting the local support he needed, so he teamed up with Senator Goodman to have the permits for the project pushed through despite local resistance. I know business and politics probably shouldn't mix, but the reality is, they do. More often than I ever realized before marrying one of the richest men in the country."

"So, to clarify, you attended the cocktail party to support your friend even though you don't necessarily support Senator Goodman in his run for governor?"

I let out a long groan. "Haven't I already said that? These questions seem totally irrelevant. Have you found out what happened to Zarek?"

Agent Stanwell paused. It felt like he was watching for my reaction, although I couldn't imagine why. "Mr. Woodson died as the result of ingesting a lethal toxin that had been added to his drink."

I cringed as I remembered Zarek's last minutes and the frenzied attempts to save him. Given the painful way he died, I'd expected poison might have been involved. "Do you know who did it? Do you know who killed Zarek?"

He leaned forward slightly, his dark eyes boring into mine. "I was hoping you could answer that question."

"Me?" I asked in a high, squeaky voice. "How would I know who killed Zarek?"

"Security cameras show an individual retrieving a vial, which we believe to have been the one containing the toxin, from your purse."

I gasped. "My purse? There must be a mistake. I can assure you, I didn't have a thing to do with Zarek's murder, and I didn't bring a vial of poison to the party. As I stated before, Zarek was a friend. Why would I kill him?"

"I don't know. Why would you?"

I blew out a breath. "I wouldn't." I looked the man in the eye. "Are you accusing me of something?"

"Should I be?"

"No," I spat. "This is ridiculous. I would never kill Zarek, or anyone else, for that matter."

"We do have the video," he reminded me.

"If you have a video of someone taking a vial from my purse, you must know whoever retrieved it wasn't me."

"The room was dark and the individual stayed in the shadows. All we really have is an image of someone retrieving the vial. It could have been anyone."

That didn't sound right at all. "Was this person tall or short? Thin or stocky? If you could make out enough to know the purse in question was mine, you must have some idea what this person looked like."

"From the image on the tape, the person could very well have been you."

Well, wasn't that fantastic! "There were a lot of women at the party." I paused to further consider the idea. "And there was a lot of security last night. A ridiculous amount. Perhaps the real killer didn't want to risk getting caught with the vial, so he or she slipped it into my purse and retrieved it later."

Agent Stanwell paused, in an attempt, I was sure, to intimidate me. He narrowed his gaze and steepled his fingers as he continued to stare at me. I felt like squirming but sat perfectly still as I waited for him to go on. The longer he paused, the tenser I became. I tightened my hands on the arms of the chair I was sitting on as I struggled to push down the urge to freak out just a tiny bit. What had happened to Zarek was horrific, and the thought that I might have played even an unwilling role in his death left me devastated.

After several minutes of total silence that had me longing to crawl out of my skin, he glanced at the purse sitting on the floor next to my feet. "I assume that's the purse you were carrying last evening?"

"It is." I nodded.

Agent Stanwell reached for it. "May I?"

I hesitated just for a moment before passing it to him. The last thing I wanted to do was to appear defensive, which would make it seem as if I really did have something to hide. Agent Stanwell took the purse from my outstretched hand and began to look through it. "If someone other than you or your husband used your purse to transport the toxin through security, we'll need to narrow down the timeline a bit. Can you remember the last time you completely emptied this purse, either to change bags or to find a lost item?"

"Thursday late afternoon," I said with conviction.

Agent Stanwell picked my wallet out of the purse and set it on the table between us. He looked at me. "I'm going to need you to be specific. Include as many details as come to mind."

Okay, that seemed an odd request, but everything about this was odd, so what the heck. I let my mind wander to the day in question. If he wanted details, I'd give him details. "My mom likes to spend time with my daughter, Catherine, so I try to drop her off for an hour or two a couple of times a week. On Thursday I had errands to take care of, so I left Catherine at my parents' place while I was in town. When I returned to pick her up, Catherine was fussier than usual. I figured it was because she's been teething, so I decided to rub some of the gel I got from the pediatrician on her gums. I was sure I'd put the tube of gel in my purse, but for the life of me, I couldn't find it. I emptied out my entire bag looking for it. In the end, my mother saved the day with a Popsicle."

Agent Stanwell paused from his examination of my bag and looked up at me. "And after you left your parents' house?"

"I went home. I was home all evening with my husband, Zak, Zak's honorary grandmother, Nona, Catherine, and the two teens who live with us, Alex Bremmerton and Scooter Sherwood."

"Am I to assume your husband and yourself, your baby, your grandmother, and your two wards are the sum total of the people who reside in your home on a full-time basis?"

Weird question, but okay. "Yes. The individuals mentioned make up the residents of the house."

"Go on," he said as he returned his attention to my bag. "Was there anyone else in the house on Thursday evening? A guest? Perhaps a neighbor?"

"No. Just the family."

"What about Friday?"

"Friday was a busy day," I answered as Stanwell set Catherine's bottle on the table next to my wallet. "A very busy day. It started early, around six a.m. I got up and made breakfast for Scooter, who was picked up by his father on Friday morning. Scooter lives with us, but he's trying to establish a relationship with his father, so he visits him during school holidays. Friday was the first day of winter break, so Scooter went on a short trip with his father. He'll be home in time for Christmas."

"And Mr. Sherwood? Was he at any time alone in your home or alone with your purse?"

I shook my head. "My purse was in the closet in my bedroom. Scooter's dad never even came inside the house. Scooter was watching for him from the window, and when he pulled into the drive, Scooter ran out to meet him."

"Is that normally the manner in which Mr. Sherwood picks up his son?"

I nodded. "Yes. When he picks him up. A lot of the time Zak will have his pilot fly Scooter to Los Angeles, where his father lives." I hesitated. "Mr. Sherwood wasn't at Zarek's party. He couldn't have killed him. I don't see why you need this much information about someone who can't possibly be considered a suspect."

Agent Stanwell looked up from rummaging through my purse. "At this point I'm just trying to establish a timeline for your day on Friday. If you emptied your purse on Thursday afternoon and the vial was taken from your purse at the party on Friday evening, that twenty-four-hour period, give or take, is the window in which the vial was placed in your purse. If we can determine when it was placed in your purse, maybe we can figure out who killed Mr. Woodson."

I was pretty sure the vial hadn't been slipped into my purse during the course of the day, and I still didn't understand the need for so much detail, but rambling on as he seemed to want me to do was a lot better than sitting in silence while he stared at me, so I continued. "So after Scooter left, I woke Catherine. I changed her diaper, then took her downstairs for breakfast. As I said, I had a busy day planned, so Zak arranged to be home to finish putting up our Christmas decorations and to keep an eye on Catherine. Before I left for the day, he wanted to run to his office at Zimmerman Academy, the private school we own and operate, to pick up some files he planned to work on over the break, so I got Catherine up and fed."

"Who else was in the house at that point?" Agent Stanwell asked.

"Just Nona and Alex. Both were still asleep."

He sat back in his chair with my purse still in his lap. "Go on."

"Catherine was just finishing her breakfast when Alex came downstairs. I was supposed to meet my mother, Madison Montgomery Donovan, and the chairperson of the local events committee, Hillary Spain, at Rosie's for a breakfast meeting regarding the annual Hometown Christmas. My mother is the chairperson of that event this year, and it seems like everything that can go wrong has gone wrong, so I've been trying to help out where I can. Anyway, Alex knew I needed to shower and dress, so she volunteered to get Catherine dressed. She's so good with her. I don't know how I'd manage without her."

"So you went up to shower, Alex saw to your daughter's needs, and your grandmother was still sleeping."

"Yes, that's correct."

"And your purse was still in the closet?"

"It was."

He set several items from my purse on the table. "Please continue."

"By the time I'd showered and dressed, Zak was back and Nona was awake. Zak and Nona were sitting at the kitchen counter chatting and Alex had gone upstairs to get ready for a friend who was coming over to help out with Santa's Sleigh."

"Santa's Sleigh?"

"It's a community service Alex founded a few years ago. She and some of her friends solicit donations to provide Christmas gifts and food baskets for the community's less-fortunate residents. It's a big commitment. Not only does Alex have to identify the families, she has to ascertain their specific needs, seek donations to meet those needs, wrap the gifts, and distribute them on the twenty-third." I stopped talking when I noticed Agent Stanwell had stopped what he was doing and was just staring at me. "Sorry. I guess that's more detail than you want. I'm just so darn proud of her."

"It sounds as if you should be. The project is a wonderful idea."

I smiled and finally began to relax.

"So, after you found your husband and his grandmother chatting in the kitchen…?"

"I kissed Zak, Nona, and Catherine goodbye, then headed out for my breakfast meeting."

"Which was held at Rosie's?" Agent Stanwell verified.

"Yes. Rosie's is a café that's very popular with the local crowd."

"And you had your purse with you at that time?"

I nodded. "Are you looking for something specific?" I glanced at the purse he still held.

"No. I'm just checking for evidence that might help us determine who put the vial in your purse if you didn't. Please go on. You had just arrived at Rosie's…"

I nodded, and Stanwell returned his attention to my purse. He seemed to be looking in the lining. I doubted he'd find anything in there, but whatever. "I hung up the purse along with my heavy jacket on the rack behind the hostess station. My mom and Hillary were already at the table when I arrived, so I sat down in the booth next to my mom and ordered coffee and a muffin. We discussed the problems we were having with some of the vendors, went over some possible options, made a few decisions, and Hillary left. I chatted with my mother for a bit longer about our plans for the upcoming holiday and then we left as well."

"Did you have your eyes on your purse the entire time you were in the restaurant?"

"No," I admitted. "I hang my coat and purse on that rack all the time. Everyone does. I've never had a problem. This is a small town. Generally speaking, neighbors trust neighbors to respect their possessions.

Besides, the hostess knows the locals and helps to keep an eye on things."

"And the name of the hostess?"

"Jennifer Sandoval. She works the weekday breakfast shift. I'm sure she can verify that I was there on Friday morning if you need proof of what I'm telling you."

Stanwell pulled one of Catherine's bibs from my bag and seemed to study it before he set it aside with the other items on the table. "After you left Rosie's when did you next look through the contents of your purse?"

"After we ate. I had to locate my keys and my sunglasses. I can't claim I looked at every item in my purse. When you have a baby, you end up carrying around a lot of stuff, which I guess you've figured out by now. I can say for sure I didn't notice a vial of any sort when I searched around for my keys and glasses."

Agent Stanwell took a pen from my bag and clicked it open and closed. "What did you do next?"

"I went to the Christmas tree lot run by the high school athletic program. My friend Levi Denton is in charge of the fund-raiser and I wanted to see if he was able to work out the problem he was having with his second tree delivery. He got the first load all right, but the second load had been held up for almost five days. When I arrived, he was on the phone. He'd received confirmation that the trees were on the way, and he really wanted to be there when they arrived so he could confirm he had the correct trees in the correct number. But he was supposed to take his wife, Ellie, to the doctor, so he was torn about what to do."

"Ellie is sick?"

"Pregnant. Very pregnant. I offered to take her to the doctor. I left right away and headed to the boathouse where they live."

"And the purse? Where was it while you were speaking to Mr. Denton?"

"On the floor of the car on the passenger side."

"Was the car locked?"

"It wasn't, but I was only at the lot for a couple of minutes."

The agent removed my phone from the bottom of my bag and held it up. "Do you mind if I take a look?"

"Knock yourself out," I said, even though I just wanted this to be over.

"What did you do after you left the tree lot?" Stanwell returned my attention to the story I was telling.

"So I drove to the boathouse to get Ellie. She has a son, Eli, so I loaded him into the car while she grabbed what she needed. When we arrived at the doctor's office, I volunteered to sit in the waiting room with Eli while she had her checkup. She's having a girl. She and Levi still haven't settled on a name for her, but they're both pretty excited about the little darling."

"I imagine they are." He seemed to be looking through my photos. I wanted to ask what photos of my family had to do with this murder investigation, but he spoke before I could say anything. "Please go on. Did you bring your purse inside with you?"

"No," I answered. "Ellie had brought a diaper bag with toys and snacks in it for Eli, so between him and the diaper bag, my hands were full."

"And the purse was left unattended in an unlocked car?"

"It was," I confirmed. "But I tucked it under a baby blanket that was on the back seat."

Agent Stanwell left my photo app and began looking through my texts. If I'd had something to hide, I'd be pretty freaked out about now, but my texts were about as boring as any texts could be.

"After the doctor, what then?" he asked.

"I took Ellie and Eli home and then I headed over to Zoe's Zoo, the wild and domestic rescue and rehabilitation shelter I own and operate with my manager, Jeremy Fisher, and our employees, Tiffany Middleton Walden and Aspen Wood. Since I welcomed Catherine into my life, I haven't been able to spend as much time at the shelter as I'd like, but I try to check in when I can, and Jeremy had taken custody of an injured mountain lion the day before and I wanted to check on how things were going."

"You had your purse with you when you visited the shelter?"

I nodded. "I brought it in and set it on my desk. Then I walked through the place with Jeremy so he could catch me up on our new arrivals."

"And who had access to your office while you were there?"

I narrowed my gaze. "My door wasn't locked. It never is because the entire staff needs to have access to it at times, but there's no way any of them would poison Zarek." I made a face. "It must be a terrible way to die."

Agent Stanwell shot me a look of sympathy. "Yes, I imagine it was. Which is why we need to catch the person who did this horrible thing."

"I agree. I'll help you in any way I can."

"Could anyone other than your staff have entered your office while you were at the shelter?"

I lifted one shoulder. "I suppose if there was a customer on site who asked to use the bathroom. It's down the same hallway as my office. I don't remember anyone else being in the building while I was there, but I can ask Aspen, who was at the front desk."

"I'll need contact information for all of your employees," Stanwell said as he logged into the contacts list on my phone.

I nodded reluctantly. "Are you sure I can't help you find something? If you just tell me what you're after, I can probably steer you right to it."

"It's fine. I'm just looking for something to pop as being relevant. After you took the tour with your manager, what then?"

"Tiffany came to find us to let us know she'd received an animal cruelty call."

"Animal cruelty?" His lips tightened. That made me like him for the first time.

"There were two dogs who'd been tied up behind a house just outside of the town limits for the past two days. The neighbor who called said she hadn't seen the owner feed the dogs in all that time, and she definitely didn't think the dogs had been let in, even at night. Jeremy and I have a policy that either he or I respond to animal cruelty calls. The thing is, you just never know what might happen when you confront a neglectful owner, and we don't want to put either Tiffany or Aspen into a potentially dangerous, volatile situation. Jeremy had a day-care group coming for a tour in less than an hour, so I volunteered to go. To tell you the truth, I wanted to have the opportunity to give the owner of the dogs a piece of my mind."

Agent Stanwell set my phone on the table with the other things he'd taken out of my purse. He seemed to be studying me, which was making me extremely uncomfortable. Again, I wondered what was really going on. I've been involved in a lot of murder investigations in my time, and this had to be the most absurd interview I'd ever been a part of.

Chapter 2

"Are you sure you need this much detail?" I asked again. "It seems like most of what I'm telling you is pretty irrelevant to what occurred last night."

The man narrowed his gaze. "Sometimes the particulars are important. Other times, not so much. Still, I'd like you to provide as much detail as possible."

I shrugged. "If you say so."

"You responded to the animal cruelty call. What happened when you got there?"

"I found the dogs tied up, as the neighbor had reported. I knocked on the door, but there wasn't an answer. I walked next door to question the neighbor further. She hadn't seen the man who owned the dogs for a couple of days but assumed he must be around somewhere if he left his dogs tied up. I went back to the man's home. I knocked again, and when there still was no answer, I left a note on the door, letting him know where his dogs would be, loaded them into the back seat of my car, and took them to the shelter."

"And your purse? Where was it during this house call?"

"Sitting on the passenger seat of my car."

"Was the purse left unattended when you went to speak to the neighbor?"

I let out a groan. "It was. Like I said, I left it on the seat of the car, and before you ask, yes, the car was unlocked. I even left my keys in the ignition."

He appeared to be trying to suppress a grin, though in my opinion there was nothing funny about this interview. "So, just to be clear, you didn't have cause to look inside your purse after returning to your vehicle?"

I shook my head. "I had my sunglasses on and, as I stated, the key was in the ignition, so once I'd loaded the dogs I took them directly to the Zoo. I was supposed to pick up Nona and Alex, so I didn't have a lot of time to do much except drop the dogs off. Jeremy, Tiffany, and Aspen took charge of the dogs and got them fed, watered, and settled."

"And your purse? Did you take it out of the vehicle at all during the transfer of possession of the dogs?"

"No. It was still on the seat, and the keys were still in the ignition. I was only inside the shelter for a minute before coming back outside with the others, so I suppose it's possible someone slipped the vial into my purse while the car was in the parking lot, but I doubt it. The school group had come and gone by the time I came back with the dogs, so the place was pretty deserted. We have a large parking lot, which on this particular day was empty except for the vehicles owned by the shelter employees. I think I would have noticed another car, or even someone on foot, approaching."

"But you were inside the building and the car was totally unattended for a short period of time?"

"Yes," I admitted.

Agent Stanwell took the last few things out of my purse and set them on the table. When it was empty, he turned it upside down and shook it. I tried to disguise my shock. "And after you left the animals?"

"I headed home. I was supposed to pick Nona up and take her into town. Friday is lunch and bingo day at the senior center and she doesn't like to miss it. After I dropped her off there, I took Alex to the airport in Bryton Lake. She has a friend visiting for a few weeks, so we went to pick her up."

"And this friend: does he or she have a name?"

I hesitated as he took a small penlight out of his pocket and began to take a closer look at the interior of my purse.

"Ms. Zimmerman. Do you know the name of your ward's friend?"

I grimaced. "Can you keep a secret?"

He looked up and then lifted a brow.

"Yes, I guess you can. The friend Alex has staying with us is Shawna Jennings."

He seemed satisfied with my answer, yet I wasn't sure why he would be. "Shawna Jennings, the country singer," he confirmed.

"Yes."

"And how does your ward happen to know Shawna Jennings, the country singer? If I remember correctly, she lives in Nashville."

I nodded. "Shawna does live in Nashville. With her mother," I added, even though I wasn't certain that piece of information was relevant. "Alex met Shawna when they both went to the same private school for gifted students, before Alex moved in with us. Alex is a very bright young woman, so even though Shawna is three years older, they were in the same grade. Alex and Shawna both had difficult home situations and bonded. They've remained friends, although with Shawna's busy life, they haven't seen each other in quite a while."

"Why is she here now? I thought I read something about her going on a Christmas tour."

Hmm. I was surprised he knew that much about Shawna. It seemed country music fans came in all shapes and sizes. "It was canceled. Shawna is totally burned out. Her mother, who acts as her agent, seems to have her booked every minute of every day. Shawna just wanted a quiet Christmas. She wanted to watch it snow and maybe have some time to reflect. She mentioned as much to Alex, so she invited her here, to spend the holiday with us. But you can't tell anyone she's here. If the press finds out, we'll have paparazzi climbing our walls for a peek. The poor thing will never get the rest she wants and deserves if others find out where she is."

"Don't worry. Unless I have reason to question her in an official capacity, I think I can leave her name out of my report." He smiled as he made additional notes. "Describe to me what went on while you were at the airport. Did you take your purse into the terminal?"

I shook my head. "Zak had arranged for his pilot to fly Shawna here. Alex and I picked her up on the

30

private-use airstrip. I did get out of the car to help Shawna with her luggage, but my vehicle was within my sight the entire time."

He leaned back in his chair, momentarily abandoning his investigation into the contents of my purse. "And what did you do after you left the airport?"

"I took Alex and Shawna back to the house. After we carted all her luggage inside, I made sure the girls had everything they needed and then went back into town to pick up Nona. I parked outside the senior center and ran in to let her know I was there. I did take my keys with me, but I left my purse in the car. But only for a few minutes."

"Was the car locked?"

"No," I admitted. "But I was only inside for maybe five minutes at the most."

"It wouldn't take long to slip a vial into your purse. Do you take Nona to bingo every Friday?"

"Yes. Mostly. I told you, she doesn't like to miss it."

"And do you pick her up at the same time each week?"

I nodded again.

"And do you always leave your purse in the car and the car door unlocked when you pick her up?"

"I do." I sighed. I wasn't at all happy that he was making me look and feel like an idiot. "I usually have Catherine with me, so my hands are full. I don't need the purse for the short time I'm inside, so why bother with it? I usually just slip my keys in my pocket, grab my baby, and go inside."

"So someone who's a local, someone who knows your routines and habits, could anticipate that your purse would be left in the parking area of the senior center unattended at what, three o'clock?"

"Three thirty, but yes. If someone had been watching me and knew my habits, that would be the perfect time to slip the vial into my purse. But I'm still having a hard time with the idea that someone would actually do such a thing. Are you very certain the cameras showed what you think they did? Could there have been another purse involved? A purse other than mine?"

Agent Stanwell seemed to ignore my question and continued with the interview. "And after you picked up your grandmother, did you look inside your purse?"

I closed my eyes to suppress a groan. "No. I tossed the purse onto the back seat because Nona would be sitting on the passenger seat. We went directly home. I threw my purse on the kitchen table, then went upstairs to spend some time with Catherine before I had to get ready for the cocktail party. After that I changed my clothes, and Zak and I headed to the Woodson estate."

Agent Stanwell began picking up the items he'd put on the table and returned them to the purse one at a time. "Did you look inside your purse at any point after the senior center?"

I shook my head. "No. Zak drove, so I didn't need my keys. It was dark, so I didn't need my sunglasses. You know, I almost didn't bring the purse with me at all, but at the last minute I grabbed it. When we arrived at the party I handed over my purse and jacket to a maid."

He continued replacing my possessions, looking closely at each one as he did. "It appears the last time you even looked inside your purse before handing it to the maid at the cocktail party was at Rosie's, after you ate."

I took a minute to think about it. "No, my keys were in my purse when I left the shelter the first time. They were right on top, so I didn't have to dig around at all, but I did open the bag."

Agent Stanwell stopped what he was doing. He frowned as he sat staring at me.

"Is there a problem?" I asked.

He held up the purse. "It's occurred to me this seems all wrong if this is the bag you brought to the party. It's a designer bag, and I imagine it was fairly expensive, but it isn't dressy. Given that the cocktail party was a dressy affair, why didn't you change purses for a dressier option?"

I laughed. "It's obvious you don't know me at all. Before Catherine was born, I didn't even carry a purse. I had a backpack I lugged around sometimes, but mostly I just kept my car keys, credit card, driver's license, and a little bit of cash in my pockets. Then Catherine was born, and I had all sorts of paraphernalia to cart around, so I bought a purse that was big enough to accommodate bottles, a change of clothes for the baby, and a few other necessities. The purse you've been looking through so thoroughly is the only one I own. Anyone who knows me knows that. In fact, I'm teased for it quite often. I guess it isn't the norm for the wives of men who have as much money as Zak to own only one purse, but seriously, you only really need one."

Stanwell nodded. "I suppose that's true."

"Is this interview being helpful at all?" I asked, doubt evident in my voice.

"I think so. I now have a feel for when the toxin might have been slipped into your bag and why the killer chose you out of all the guests who were invited to the party as his mule."

"You do?"

"You don't change the purse you carry to go with each outfit, the way many, if not most, women do. You have a somewhat regular routine on Friday afternoons. And you're the most careless woman with your purse of any woman I've ever met."

"Hey! I'm not careless."

He lifted his eye. "You leave your purse unattended a great deal of the time."

"That doesn't make me careless; it makes me trusting. Besides, as you can see, there isn't anything of real value in it."

"What about your wallet?"

"I have only one credit card with a low limit that can be canceled if stolen. I carry a bit of cash, but certainly not a lot."

Agent Stanwell picked up my wallet, which he hadn't rummaged through when he removed it from the purse, and opened the front clasp. I felt like I should point out that he was invading my privacy big-time, but he'd already riffled through my phone, so what difference did this make? "I've never been at all concerned that someone might steal my purse, although I admit it never occurred to me that someone would put something into it when I wasn't looking rather than taking something out. I suppose, given the circumstances, an argument could be made that I should keep better track of the darn thing."

"That might be a good idea." Stanwell pulled out my driver's license and looked at it. "I suspect the person who slipped the vial into your bag knows you well enough to know your routine. I'm hoping we can narrow in on a suspect who knows you that well and had a reason to kill Mr. Woodson."

I thought about that. Eventually, I shook my head. "No. That doesn't feel right. Your premise is that someone who knows me—someone who knows my routine—slipped the vial of poison into my purse at some point on Friday knowing I would carry it to the party. The problem with that theory is that someone who knew me well enough to know my routine would know it was equally likely I wouldn't bring the purse to the party at all. Before having Catherine and buying the purse, I just slipped my phone and a lipstick into Zak's jacket pocket when we went out. Now that I've begun carrying the purse, I bring it with me a lot of the time, but we're still talking about a fifty-fifty chance. If someone wanted to ensure that the vial showed up at the party, they wouldn't have wanted to depend on me to show up with the purse."

"What are you saying?"

"That the only thing that makes sense is that someone slipped the vial into my bag after we arrived at the party."

That seemed to get Stanwell's attention. "Someone like the valet?"

I nodded as he returned my license to my wallet and my wallet to my purse. "Exactly. After we arrived, the valet opened the door for me. I reached in, grabbed my purse, and got out. It was icy, so he offered me a hand, which I accepted. I had the bag over my shoulder, and it opens on the top. It would have been easy for him to slip the vial into the bag when he reached around to close the door behind me.

Maybe the valet was working with someone on the inside. Someone who for some reason I can't begin to comprehend was unable to bring the vial into Zarek's home directly."

Agent Stanwell caressed his chin. It appeared he was considering my theory. "Did you come into contact with anyone other than the valet between the time you arrived at the party and the time you surrendered your bag to the maid?"

"There was a man at the door. His name is Carson. I don't remember his last name, but Zak would know. He was introduced to me as Zarek's business partner. He was greeting folks, and he shook both my hand and Zak's. I didn't notice him slip anything into my bag, but I wasn't watching for anyone to do it. After he greeted us, he steered us toward the maid who was taking the coats and purses. She was stationed just inside the entry." I blew out a breath. None of this made sense to me. "So what now?" I asked, as he sat drumming his fingers on the table.

He glanced at his watch, then returned the last of my things to my purse. He handed the purse back to me. "Let's discuss motive. I understand you're a lifelong resident of Aston Falls."

I smiled proudly. "Born and raised."

"Tell me about Mr. Woodson and his resort. You said he'd been courting the senator because of problems he was having with local support for his project."

"Zarek met with resistance from two angles. There were those who welcomed the idea of a new resort but balked at the exclusivity of this project, and then there were the environmentalists who didn't want to see any more of the mountain developed. The environmentalists in the area are a strong group with a lot of influence, so Zarek realized he'd need help to get the permits he'd need to proceed, which was where Senator Goodman came in."

Stanwell picked up a pen that he began tapping on the table in front of him in what seemed to be a habitual manner. "Am I to assume you support the project?"

"No, I don't. I'm an avid skier, and there's a part of me that would welcome a luxury resort like the one Zarek was proposing, but I care about the environment, and I found myself agreeing with those who made a case for the area already being overdeveloped."

"Which would result in…" Stanwell let the words dangle.

I adjusted my position in the chair while I thought about my response. "My main concern is the impact a new resort would have on the wildlife in the area. As it is, with the development that's taken place over the past fifty years, wilderness areas once teeming with wildlife has been carved up to provide ski runs and infrastructure for the five ski areas we already have. The result is a loss of available space for the animals that remain. The more the land's developed, the more likely it is that wildlife that once lived far away from humans will be forced into populated areas. While I love the challenge of a new ski run, to me, the animals come first. That's why Zoe's Zoo came about."

"And the others who attended the cocktail party? Did they support the project?"

I lifted a shoulder. "Some did and some didn't. The community as a whole is split. There are those who argue that the development of a world-class ski resort would bring much-needed jobs to the area. An argument can also be made that an elite resort geared toward an upper-class clientele would provide a boost to our overall economy. I imagine both of those assertions have a basis in fact. But there are those, like me, who are more concerned for the wildlife and environment that surrounds us. We worry about our way of life, which is pretty causal and kick back. Personally, I'm not interested in turning the area near Ashton Falls into another resort catering to the super-rich."

"It's true that areas that attract an upper-class skier bring with them five-star restaurants, expensive boutiques, and an out-of-control housing market."

"Exactly. Many of the folks who live and work here now moved to Ashton Falls in the first place for its small-town charm. They came to own homes and raise families. Zak and I have visited small towns that went the exclusive resort route, and in the end the people who work there can't afford to live there. A lot of these resorts have to bus employees in from other towns where regular folks making regular wages can afford to live."

Stanwell twisted his lips to the side in a half smile, half sneer. "That seems like a unique attitude from one of the upper-class folks the resort is hoping to attract."

"I realize my mother and my husband have a lot of money, but that isn't the way I was brought up. I'm just a small-town girl, and a small-town lifestyle is what I want for myself and my children."

"From your knowledge of the individuals who attended the cocktail party, who do you think had the most motive to want Mr. Woodson dead?"

Hmm. That was a good question. "Zarek didn't invite obvious opponents of his project, which I suppose is understandable, although a handful of rich and powerful men and women in the community who don't support the project managed to find a way in. I assume they went to Goodman directly for an invite."

"Let's start there. Who was there who might not support the resort idea?"

"Travis Zukerman, for one. Travis has been a very vocal advocate for a zero-growth policy for this area. He owns a hundred acres on the west shore of the lake. He's bright and well educated and very passionate about his cause. He also has a lot of money and the political clout that goes with that. I doubt Zarek would have invited him to the party, but Travis has enough clout to come up with an invitation anywhere he wants to go."

I watched as Stanwell took a small notepad out of his pocket and jotted down his name. Then he looked at me again.

"Alisha Cobalter was someone else who seemed unlikely to have been a guest chosen by Zarek. She doesn't have a full-time residence here, but she does have a weekend home in Ashton Falls. She's an environmental attorney in Bryton Lake. I guess you could say she spends maybe a third of her time in town. She's the director for the local watchdog agency for the environment. Like Travis, she's smart, driven, and passionate. And she also has quite a bit of money at her disposal. She likes to sue environmental offenders, but I don't see her as a killer, though she has a mean streak. I'm kind of scared of her myself."

"Scared why?"

"Without meaning to, I'm afraid Zak and I have ended up on her naughty list a time or two. Most recently was when we decided to expand our boathouse. I own it, and the Dentons live in it. Before the expansion, it was really just a studio with a loft: not nearly large enough for a growing family. I love having my best friends living right next door, so rather than having them move out and me having to find a new tenant, I chose to expand. Zak and I got all the proper permits from the county and the building department, but it didn't occur to us that we ought to get Alisha's blessing before we did anything. Not that it was legally required, but looking back, it might have saved us some grief if we had. By the time she found out about the expansion it was well underway. Talk about having an angry, angry woman on our hands! She threatened us with all sorts of stuff, but in the end, as smart as she is, Zak is smarter, and he convinced her it was in her best interests to back off."

"What exactly was her problem with your expansion?"

"Land coverage. As I mentioned, Travis, Alisha, and a few others want to see zero growth and zero loss of natural land coverage. In Alisha's mind, our expansion onto previously uncovered real estate was as bad as if we'd built a whole new house. And maybe it is the same thing. I know I didn't look at it that way. And while I understand there are neighborhoods where the houses have been built so close together you can barely walk between them, which I suppose isn't ideal, we have a lot of vacant land on our estate, so I don't think the expansion will have all that much of an impact on the environment as a whole. Of course, in Alisha's eyes we're probably just another rich, entitled couple who did what we wanted to do without giving a single thought to the overall picture."

"Are you suggesting you believe this woman might kill a man and make it look as if you'd done it as some sort of revenge?"

I shook my head. "Revenge, no. I'm not saying anything other than that Alisha is someone you may at least want to have a chat with. I suspect she's absolutely livid over Zarek's project. She's been in Ashton Falls since the first of the month and plans to stay through the first of the year, so you should be able to track her down."

"All right. Were there any other guests you feel might have a reason to want Mr. Woodson out of the way?"

"Garrison Ford. He's the owner of Bear Mountain, the largest ski resort in Ashton Falls. While Zarek's resort was going to be small in comparison, I could see how it would hurt Bear Mountain if he skimmed the richest guests off the top." I sat back and looked at the agent. "That's really all I can think of right now."

He nodded.

"So are we done?"

"You're free to go, but I'm going to need to speak to your husband."

Chapter 3

As it turned out, Agent Stanwell spent almost as much time interviewing Zak as he had me. By the time we got home half the day was gone. Not exactly the way I'd planned to spend my Saturday, but oh well, what are you going to do?

I checked in with Alex and Shawna, who expressed their intention of hanging out in the house wrapping gifts for Santa's Sleigh while they watched Christmas movies and played with the kittens Alex was fostering. It sounded like a nice, relaxing day. Catherine was visiting my parents until later in the afternoon and Nona had spent the night in town with a friend, which just left Zak and me to entertain ourselves. It wasn't often that Zak and I had alone time, so we wanted to take advantage of the childfree day to finish up our Christmas shopping. But first, we decided, we'd treat ourselves to a nice lunch at the steakhouse that had recently opened on the lake.

"So, what do you make of Agent Stanwell?" I asked Zak as we drove through town.

"I think he knows more than he's letting on, which is fine, I suppose, considering it's his job to find out what we know but not necessarily bring us up to speed."

I frowned. "Yeah. It's frustrating not to be working with Salinger. Where is he anyway?"

"It could be he's been told to take a back seat while the fed does his interviews. I'm not sure why the FBI is involved in the murder of a local businessman, but maybe it has something to do with Senator Goodman attending the party. My guess is Salinger will get involved after the fed's done."

"I hope so. Agent Stanwell made me very uncomfortable, and the interview was so bizarre, I almost felt he was after something other than the information he specifically asked for."

"What do you mean?"

I turned slightly. "For one thing, the amount of detail he seemed to be after made no sense. If he wanted to figure out when someone might have slipped the vial into my purse, it seems like he could have taken a much more direct route with his questions. It was more like he was trying to trip me up, to trick me into saying what he was really looking for."

Zak turned onto the lake road. "You think he was fishing?"

I shrugged. "Maybe. And then there was the whole security camera thing. He said he had a video of someone pulling a vial from my purse, but my coat and purse were in the closet with everyone else's. Yes, it was a large closet, almost the size of a small bedroom, but still, who has security cameras inside a closet?"

Zak frowned. "Good point."

"The entire time I was talking with him, I had this feeling he was trying to steer the interview toward some predetermined outcome. An outcome, if I had to guess, that had absolutely nothing to do with my purse or its use as a method for delivering the poison."

Zak slowed the truck. "Maybe we should call Salinger. Get his take on things. Even if the sheriff's office isn't the lead agency on the investigation, it would seem he'd know something about what's really going on."

"I'll call him on his personal cell," I said. "That way he won't get into trouble for speaking to us if Stanwell happens to be in his office when I reach him."

As it turned out, Salinger didn't pick up, so I left a message letting him know I needed to speak to him as soon as he could return my call. In the meantime, Zak and I went ahead and had lunch.

******

The Lake House, as it was appropriately named, was a large log building perched on the water just south of Ashton Falls. On the wall to the left of the windows was a river-rock fireplace that reached three stories, and to the right was a slightly raised platform with a baby grand piano. Today a man dressed in a black tux was playing holiday songs as diners enjoyed the fire and the view while dining on entrees that included pulled pork or sliced steak sandwiches, mile-high Kobe beef burgers, or lamb stew.

"This is so nice and very relaxing," I said as I paused to appreciate the twenty-foot tree decorated with white lights and red and gold balls. "I've been wanting to try the food here, but this isn't somewhere I'd bring Catherine."

"I agree," Zak said as he looked over the menu. "This wouldn't be the best place to bring a baby or even a young child. I heard the steak and potato chowder is really good, as is the warm beet and grapefruit salad, although the special looked pretty good as well."

After we placed our order, I looked around the room. Between the snow falling gently outside the window near our table, the fire crackling merrily in the huge fireplace, the soft piano music, and the festive yet elegant decorations, I found the spirit of the season slowly returning, despite the hectic morning we'd had. I placed my hand over Zak's and gave it a squeeze. How I truly cherished these quiet moments, when it was just the two of us. "When we leave here, we should check out the windows on Main Street. I've been so busy, I haven't had the chance, although I did want to bring Catherine to see them. Maybe we can do them twice."

"What time do you need to pick Catherine up?"

"I told my mom I'd be by around four. I was going to take Alex and Shawna into town this evening to see the lights and have dinner, but I should talk to them before I make any plans. Shawna really wants to keep a low profile while she's here. Even going out to dinner might put her at risk of being recognized."

Zak took a sip of his beer. "She doesn't appear to be the sort who'd be bothered by fanfare and attention. Any idea why she suddenly decided to hide out?"

"I spoke to her about it when we drove home from the airport. Apparently, it isn't just her fans she's hiding from but her parents as well."

Zak raised a brow. "Her parents?"

I nodded. "She told me they divorced when she was young. She didn't seem to think they were well suited and probably should never have married. She said her parents met at a neurobiology conference, attended by her father, a world-renowned neuroscientist. Her mother, a struggling country singer at the time, was appearing as a backup singer for the headliner, who was hired to perform during the Saturday night meet and greet. Shawna hinted their affair was steamy and intense but brief. By the time Shawna's mother found out she was pregnant, it was already almost over. If it weren't for Shawna, she's sure they would have gone their separate ways."

"But they didn't," Zak said.

"No. They got married instead. Her mother gave up the possibility of a career to raise her child. When they divorced a couple of years later, Shawna and her mother moved to Nashville to live with her grandmother. Shawna loved to sing even at a very young age, so her mother convinced her father to pay for singing and dance lessons. By the time she was four, she was competing with other kids in her age group, and when she was six she won a national competition."

"It seems like her story is one of following your dreams and realizing everything you ever wanted, but I'm sensing there's a *but* to come," Zak said.

"A big but. When Shawna was almost seven her mother was in an auto accident. Shawna went to live with her father while her mother was recovering. Up until then, she hadn't spent a lot of time with her father. During the four weeks Shawna lived with him, he got to know her and realized she was extremely intelligent. The scientist who'd never really been interested in his child was suddenly confronted with a prodigy. He insisted Shawna attend private schools for gifted students from that time, where her natural intelligence could be developed."

"And that's where she eventually met Alex."

"Exactly. Even though Shawna is three years older than Alex, they were in a lot of the same classes and became friends."

Zak settled back in the booth. "Go on. What happened next?"

"Shawna now had two parents who had very different goals for her. In the beginning it was a real mess, but at some point they came up with a compromise: Shawna would get a top-rate education *and* pursue her career in music. On the surface it sounds like she was afforded a wonderful opportunity, but it meant she was scheduled twenty-four seven. If she wasn't in school, she was on tour. She never even had days off, so she never had time to figure out what she wanted to do. Shawna turned eighteen a few weeks ago and has access to her own money, so she could be self-sufficient. For the first time, she won't have to do what her parents worked out for her. She told Alex her father is pushing hard for her to give up her singing career and focus full time on academics, while her mother is after her to leave school entirely and put all her energy into her singing career."

Zak's expression softened. "Poor kid. No wonder she wanted some time to get away from it all."

"My sense is that Shawna loves both her parents and doesn't want to anger either of them. I also think she enjoys both school and her career, but she's being pulled in two very different directions and it might be time to choose one or the other. Or even something different altogether. She told her mom she couldn't do the tour she'd planned for her because she was spending Christmas with her dad and told her dad she couldn't go to the conference he wanted her to attend because she was going on tour with her mom. What she really did was come here."

"Don't you think her parents will figure out she's lying to both of them?" Zak asked.

"Shawna insists they no longer speak to each other, so she doubts they'll ever find out. She's legally an adult and could have just told them she needed time to herself, but she didn't want to hurt either of them. She decided a lie was the kindest way to go until she can come to a decision."

We were quiet as our food was delivered. Everything looked and smelled wonderful. I'd chosen a hot seafood sandwich on a homemade roll, while Zak had gone with the lamb stew.

"Oh my gosh, this looks to die for," I said as I picked out a piece of shrimp and popped it into my mouth.

"The stew is good as well, but I should have ordered a roll to go with it."

"I'm sure it's not too late." I looked up in search of our waiter, which was when I spotted Zarek's business partner walking into the restaurant.

"The man at the hostess station—we met him at the door last night, although I never saw him again all evening, which is pretty odd."

Zak turned around to look. "Carson Amundson. You're right, it's odd that he greeted everyone at the door but didn't join us for cocktails."

My eyes narrowed. "We know he was there last night, so I wonder where he went off to." I watched as a beautiful woman dressed in a bright red angora dress joined Carson at the hostess station. The couple were shown to a table by a window.

Zak watched them, then looked back at me. "When I spoke to Alton Biswell last evening," he said, referring to a local business owner, "he did bring up that Zarek was in some sort of dispute with his business partners. He mentioned it while explaining why he'd decided not to invest in the ski project. The dispute might have something to do with what occurred last night."

I glanced toward the table where the two were engaged in what looked to be an intense conversation. "Do you know who the woman is? The one with Amundson?"

Zak shook his head. "I've never seen her before."

"I wonder if we wandered over to say hi, whether he'd introduce us."

"Are you sure you want to do that? We're here for a nice lunch, not to get even more involved in a murder investigation."

"True." I glanced at them. "But it seems like the neighborly thing to do is to offer our condolences to a man who's lost his business partner." I stood up. "We'll just stay for a moment and then return to our lunch."

I was pretty sure I heard Zak groan, but he stood up, took my hand, and led me across the restaurant.

Of course, once I found out Carson Amundson was having lunch with Senator Goodman's very beautiful publicist, I had to wonder if the meal was a friendly meeting of colleagues or a strategy session of some sort. Zak had said Zarek was engaged in a conflict with his business partners. Now it occurred to me whether one of the partners at least hadn't found a way to pursue the elite resort without the man who'd proposed the project in the first place.

I could tell Zak really wanted the few hours we had alone together to be about us, so I put those thoughts on the back burner to enjoy the afternoon with my husband.

"Maybe we should drop by the tree lot to see how Levi is doing with the fund-raiser," Zak suggested. "We haven't helped much this year. I know we've been busy, so I'd like to make a donation to the high school sports program."

"I think that's a great idea. Let's park near the fishing bridge, then walk down one side of Main Street looking at the windows until we get to the tree lot. We can chat with Levi for a few minutes, then check out the windows on the other side of the street until we get back to the truck."

Zak looked up. The snow had stopped, but the sky was dark, promising additional flakes before it was all over. "Do you have your gloves? The walk you're suggesting is at least a mile."

I pulled my red fuzzy gloves out of my pockets. "I have them. After that huge lunch, a nice long walk will do us good."

"You aren't wrong about that."

We drove to the fishing bridge and parked, and Zak took my hand in his and we started down the street. Every year, the merchants on Main Street worked together to have their windows tell a story. The story this year had to do with a little girl named Holly who left home at Christmas to find Santa to make a wish she felt was too important to communicate in a handwritten letter. Along the way she meets a lot of people and has many adventures.

"Oh, look at this one with the winter carnival," I said, plastering my face against the glass of the front window of Patrick's Home Furnishings. "I especially love the carousel."

"The spinning hot cocoa cups is pretty cute too," Zak added. "We'll definitely have to bring Catherine to see the windows. Or at least some of them. I'm not sure she has the stamina to do all thirty-two."

"I can't believe she's almost a year old. It seems like just last Christmas I was wobbling around like a penguin, trying to keep my balance on the icy sidewalks."

Zak laughed. "It was last Christmas. But yeah, I get what you're saying. As long as we're in town, I want to stop to buy some paint for the rocking horse I'm making for her. What color should I make the saddle?"

"Red. Catherine likes red. If you use green for contrast, you can tell Catherine it's her Christmas pony. I bet she'll keep it and set it out every Christmas for the rest of her life."

Zak smiled and squeezed my hand. "That would be nice. I was thinking of making one for Eli too. In fact, I'd like to make one for all the kids for their first Christmas, or in the case of Catherine and Eli, their second one."

It was nice that Zak considered Levi and Ellie's children to be part of our family. I'd always felt that way about them. I was an only child growing up, so Levi and Ellie had been like the siblings I'd always longed for. We'd spent what seemed like a lifetime as best friends, and if I had my way about it, we'd spend the rest of our time on earth that way.

By the time we made it to the tree lot the snow had stopped, and the sun had even peeked out. Ellie was sitting in a chair watching Eli as he toddled after his father, who was arranging the trees that had been delivered the previous day. The lot was decked out with lights, which, added to the holiday tunes and the fresh snow, made for a magical place to buy a tree.

"Oh good, I'm happy for some extra helping hands," Levi said, handing Zak a pair of work gloves.

"Aren't the members of the teams supposed to be helping you?" I asked when I realized it looked as if Levi was alone today.

"They are. And they have been. To a point. I had a couple of guys from the football team here earlier, but they had something much more urgent to attend to. I have another group of volunteers coming soon, but I'd like to get these trees out as soon as possible. It's been a busy day and I want to come as close to selling out as possible before we close up on noon on Christmas Eve."

"I can't believe it's just ten days until Christmas." I glanced at Eli in his little overalls and his red-and-black-plaid flannel shirt. He sure looked cute, and so very much like his daddy. "At least you have one volunteer who didn't bail on you."

Levi picked Eli up and tossed him gently into the air, which made him break out into a fit of giggles. "And what a good volunteer he's been."

"Donations are definitely up when Eli is doing the asking," Ellie agreed as she adjusted her position with a look of discomfort on her face.

"Speaking of donations…" Zak took a wad of cash out of his pocket and gave it to Eli to put in the red donation bucket.

"Are you okay?" I asked, pulling up a chair and sitting down next to Ellie.

"I'm fine. Just a few twinges."

"From your expression a minute ago, I'd say there are more than twinges going on."

Ellie lowered her voice and leaned toward me. "I've had a few contractions. They're probably nothing, and I don't want to worry Levi until I'm sure. He's already stressed out with all the problems he's had with the tree lot this year."

"If you're in labor, you need to go to the hospital."

Ellie nodded. "I will. I just want to be sure." She cringed as another contraction must have gripped her. Yep, definitely more than a twinge. "I think we've decided on a name for the baby," Ellie said after the pain passed.

My eyes grew wide. "Really? What did you pick?"

"Alya. We both like it, and it feels like it goes with Levi, Ellie, and Eli."

I hugged my best friend. "I think it's perfect. What about a middle name?"

"We decided to name her after my grandmother on my mother's side, Ellanne, which is where my mom got Ellie when I was born."

"Alya Ellanne Denton. I like it. It really is perfect."

Ellie rubbed her hand over her stomach. The poor thing. She looked so uncomfortable. I remembered feeling exactly like that a year ago, and to be honest, it wasn't something I was looking forward to repeating anytime soon.

Ellie let out a soft groan. "I'm not sure I'm in labor now, but I hope she'll be a go-getter and arrive early. I'd love to have her home and settled before Christmas, and I'd prefer she not be born on Christmas Day."

I smiled as Ellie's face reddened in response to what must be another contraction. "From that look, I'm sure she'll be here in time for Christmas. In fact, I'd be willing to bet she'll be here today. Did you get her a stocking?"

"I did. And presents too. I figure Eli can open them for his baby sister."

I was about to respond when Ellie gasped. "That's it." I stood up. "I'm letting Levi know what's going on."

"But Eli and the tree lot," Ellie began to argue before inhaling sharply.

"Zak and I can take care of both."

Ellie opened her mouth.

"No arguments," I said in a tone that left no doubt I meant what I said.

Chapter 4

I guess what they say about second babies coming sooner than first is true, because just two hours later Levi was calling to let us know that Alya Ellanne Denton had arrived, and mother and baby were doing fine. My mom had come by earlier to pick up Eli, assuring me that she was happy to watch both Eli and Catherine for as long as we needed, so I told Levi that Zak and I would see to the tree lot until closing so he could focus on his wife and new baby.

"I can't believe Levi and Ellie have two children," I said to Zak after I shared the good news. "Most of the time I feel like one child is plenty to handle."

Zak put his arm around my shoulder and pulled me close. "One child is perfect for us right now, but someday…"

I had to admit I cringed at the thought of another baby, but someday seemed doable as long as it wasn't anytime soon. Not that I didn't adore Catherine. Because I did. But it felt like my life was already being pulled in so many directions, it would be good to have some time to get used to the new normal before we expanded our family again.

"Eli sure looked cute in his little lumberjack outfit today," I commented as we stacked trees. "He has many of Ellie's features, but I think he looks more and more like Levi every day. In fact, that outfit reminded me…" My comment was interrupted by the ringing of my phone. "It's Salinger," I said before answering.

"Donovan," Sheriff Salinger said, "I was planning to call you this evening after I organized some of my notes, but I got your message and decided to call now."

"I'm glad you did. I have some questions and concerns about Agent Stanwell."

"Agent Stanwell?" Salinger asked.

"The guy from the FBI who interviewed Zak and me this morning. At least I guess he was from the FBI. I'm not sure he ever said what agency he was from, but I assumed FBI."

My words were met with silence.

"Salinger?" I asked when he failed to respond.

"I'm afraid I don't know an Agent Stanwell," Salinger finally responded. "I happened to talk with an Agent Thompson from the FBI this morning and he didn't mention anyone doing interviews in town. Are you sure this Agent Stanwell didn't give you the name of the agency he worked for?"

I glanced at Zak with what I was sure was a look of confusion on my face. "I'm pretty sure he didn't. Zak is with me. We're at the tree lot covering for Levi, who, by the way, just became a daddy for the second time, or we'd come over right away."

"I'll come to you," Salinger said. "But before I leave my office I'm going to make a few calls to see if I can find out who this Agent Stanwell is."

Suddenly, all my doubts came flooding back. I *knew* there was something off about the interview this morning. I should have listened to my gut. Of course, just because Salinger had never heard of the guy didn't mean he wasn't legit. I'd wait to find out what Salinger was able to learn before I beat myself up too badly.

"What's up?" Zak asked when I hung up the phone.

"Salinger said he's never heard of Agent Stanwell, and as far as he knew, the FBI didn't have anyone in town doing interviews today."

Zak frowned. "That's odd."

"Very odd. When we arrived at the hotel Stanwell flashed his badge, but I have to admit I didn't get a good look at it. In retrospect, I guess I should have asked for verification of who he was and who he worked for, but after what happened last night, I just assumed he was legit. He looked legit."

Zak had a scowl on his face but didn't reply immediately.

"He spoke to you for a long time," I added. "Almost as long as he spoke to me. What did you talk about?"

"He asked me about my relationship with Zarek. He wanted to know about the project Zarek was working on and whether I planned to invest in it. He seemed interested in the financial and social backgrounds of the other men and women at the party, but I didn't provide any information about them because I didn't have their permission to do so."

"It would be more appropriate for him to speak to the partygoers themselves."

"That's what I thought," Zak said. "After I expressed my unwillingness to discuss the others, he asked a lot of questions about Senator Goodman and my presence at a party held in his honor. He asked about my political views, and whether I supported his run for governor. I made it clear I preferred not to discuss my political views with a stranger and reminded him they weren't the point of the interview. The victim was Zarek, not Senator Goodman." Zak grimaced.

"What is it?"

"I'm remembering the look on his face when I pointed out that the victim was Zarek and not Goodman."

"What about the look?"

"It was a brief flash, but it almost seemed like denial."

"Denial?"

Zak shook his head. "Never mind. It isn't important. After I made it clear I wasn't going to discuss my political views, he asked about Zimmerman Academy and Zimmerman Software. I answered most of those questions, but the specific ones about the staff and even students at the Academy I wasn't comfortable answering. I replied, but I was as vague as I could be without angering him."

"I guess it isn't unusual for an FBI agent to get as much information out of a witness as he possibly can. I mean, a man died last night. Finding out who killed him should take some sort of precedence, but I understand why you were reluctant to discuss what you knew about others. Especially the staff and students at the Academy."

"I probably would have said even less if I'd suspected he wasn't who he said he was."

"He still might be legit," I reminded Zak. "Although it's odd that he never said exactly who he worked for." I tried to remember the exchange when Zak and I first arrived at the hotel. We'd received a call earlier in the morning from a man who identified himself as Agent Stanwell. He said he had some questions for us and could come to our home, or we could meet him at the hotel where he was staying. We didn't want him to come to the house where Alex, Shawna, and Catherine were, so we agreed to go to the hotel. When we arrived he flashed the badge that looked legit and asked me to come upstairs with him while Zak waited in the lobby. His questions seemed odd, but it never occurred to me he might be an imposter. "If the guy turns out not to be from the FBI or some other federal agency, what on earth was he after? The questions he asked me seemed to be almost exclusively focused on the whereabouts of my purse prior to our arrival at the party. I can't see how that information would be worth the effort he must have gone to just to find out whether I keep track of the darn thing, or if, as he pointed out, I was the most careless woman he'd ever met."

Zak chuckled.

"It's not funny."

"It's a little funny. You do leave your bag laying around unattended. We've talked about you either keeping it with you or locking it in the car trunk on many occasions."

I rolled my eyes. Zak *had* talked to me about that very thing, but that didn't mean I'd listened. I glanced toward the front of the lot. "It looks like we have customers."

He headed to the couple who had just walked onto the lot and I headed to the family who'd stopped to look at wreaths. The young couple had two boys I estimated to be around five or six, and two young girls who were in a double stroller.

"Can I help you?" I asked.

"My little sister is part of the Ashton Falls High School girls' volleyball team," the woman responded. "She told me she made some of the wreaths that were donated for the fund-raiser. I want to buy one to display at my booth for Hometown Christmas if they haven't already sold out, but after looking at what you have on display, I'm not sure which wreaths are hers."

"Hmm," I responded. "I'm just filling in today, so I have no idea if there's a list saying who made the wreaths or donated them. I suppose you could call your sister to have her describe her wreaths to you." I picked up one of the wreaths and turned it over just to make sure there wasn't additional information on the tag. "It does seem each wreath is unique, so I assume most can be traced back to the individual who made them with the right information."

"I guess I could do that. Or maybe it doesn't really matter. The kids are a lot more focused on the trees, so maybe we'll take care of that today and I can come back with my sister tomorrow or the next day."

I smiled. "That seems like a good idea. So you're going to have a booth at Hometown Christmas?"

"I'm selling fudge for the children's arts program. We're hoping to make enough to send some of our less-fortunate members to dance camp this summer."

"I heard about that fund-raiser. I think sending kids to camp is a wonderful project. How are you doing so far?"

She shrugged. "Okay, I guess. Donations are slow at this time of the year. There are just so many organizations holding fund-raisers. We don't really need the cash until the spring, so we're doing what we can with the fudge now and then trying for a larger percentage of the overall pie in February with a Valentine's dance competition. If you like to dance, you should enter. It's strictly an amateur thing."

I laughed. "I have two left feet, but I'll definitely buy some fudge and spectator tickets to the dance competition."

"If you want fudge you'd best come early. We'll sell out."

"Will you be in the community center?"

"Unfortunately, no. I guess there was a problem with the tent that the committee rented to use for the food court, so that's moving into the community center and the Santa House is going to the high school gym. There isn't enough room for all the food vendors who wanted to be near the Santa House, so some of us have to make do with outside booths. I just hope the weather is good. I really don't want to spend the entire weekend freezing my keister off."

"I heard it's supposed to be sunny next weekend. Of course, our weather is pretty unpredictable, so we'll just have to see. I hadn't heard about the food tent. That must be a new development."

"I think it is. I just got a call about the change this morning. I'll look for you next weekend. Remember, come early."

After she picked out a tree and left, I helped another young family with four children pick out a nice seven-footer that had the children jumping for joy. I felt bad for my mom, who'd volunteered to chair Hometown Christmas this year. It seemed that everything that could go wrong was. Maybe I'd talk with her about it when we picked up Catherine and Eli. I knew Mom could handle whatever was thrown at her, but it couldn't be fun to have one problem after another come up. I rang up a couple who bought two colorful wreaths and went to find Zak, who was ringing up a fifteen-footer for the couple who'd come in earlier. Our own home boasted seven trees of varying sizes thanks to my Christmas crazy husband. There was a twenty-foot tree in the entry, a smaller yet still massive tree in the living room, and smaller trees in each of the occupied bedrooms. There was even a tiny dresser-top tree in Catherine's room. I wasn't going to put one in there, but she so loved looking at the twinkling lights. Now, with seven trees in the house, I was having a heck of a time keeping my cats, Marlow and Spade, from climbing them, knocking down the bulbs, and then batting them around the room.

"Salinger is here," I said to Zak after he helped the couple load their tree. "I just saw him pull around back."

"We'll need to talk where we can still watch for customers. I wouldn't want to let Levi down. He's worked really hard on this lot, and I know he's hoping to make enough for new football uniforms."

"I saw the donation you sent in at the beginning of the month. I think he can afford the uniforms."

"Okay then, he can use the money the trees make for new gear. Let's turn up the Christmas carols a bit so we won't be overheard by folks walking by on the street."

Ever since I'd spoken to Salinger, I'd been anxious to hear what he had to say. I couldn't believe I'd allowed myself to be interviewed without making sure exactly who was asking the questions. The man had flashed a badge and was wearing a suit. He'd looked like someone who would be investigating the murder of a high-profile person.

"What do you know?" I asked as soon as Salinger parked and made his way over to where we were waiting.

"The man calling himself Agent Stanwell doesn't work for the FBI. I'm not saying he doesn't work for a legitimate federal agency, I'm only saying he doesn't work for the FBI."

"What other agency could he be with?" I asked.

"I'm not sure. I have some feelers out, but I'm still waiting to hear back. I'd be surprised, though, if a legitimate federal agency came to town and didn't at least check in with local law enforcement."

"Yeah." I sighed. "I think we've been duped."

"The FBI agent I spoke to was clear they didn't have anyone on the mountain. They plan to research the situation and may very well send someone to conduct witness interviews, but if they do, I'll be made aware of it ahead of time."

"Do you know anything about what happened to Zarek?" I asked.

"A bit. We know he died as the result of ingesting a chemical compound that's known to have a paralyzing affect. In Mr. Woodson's case, his major organs, including his lungs and heart, were paralyzed, resulting in death. The toxin is fast-acting, so it probably entered his bloodstream just minutes before he began to feel the effects. We suspect it was added to his drink. I have a list of everyone who was at the party. I'd like to go over it with the two of you. After my interviews today, I feel like I'm beginning to get a feel for what went on and where everyone stands on the issue of the resort, but I've never met most of the people on the guest list. It's hard to know who could have motive to lie." Salinger looked at Zak. "You've had occasion to at least meet if not get to know a lot of the folks who were in the room. I'd appreciate some feedback."

"And I'd be happy to provide it, but we promised Levi we'd stay until closing."

"Tomorrow, then. I have some information to verify anyway, so I'll be working late as well." Salinger began to walk away, then turned back. "So how did Ellie and the baby do?"

"They did fine," I answered. "I haven't had a chance to go by the hospital and visit yet, but Levi said everything went fine."

Salinger nodded. "Okay, then. I'll see you tomorrow."

Chapter 5

Sunday, December 16

"Good morning, sunshine," I said to Catherine the next morning. It had snowed overnight, so Zak suggested we allow the dogs to run free around the fenced-in area of the estate rather than taking them for a long walk. That sounded fine with me, given the fact that Catherine had slept in.

"Da."

"Daddy is making pancakes. As soon as we get you dressed, we'll go down and have some. I know they're your favorite."

Catherine stood up in her crib. "Lele," she said, and pointed toward the doorway behind me. Charlie was standing in the threshold.

"It looks like Charlie wants to stay inside where it's warm. Not that I blame him. Let's get you changed and then both of you can have pancakes."

Catherine grinned.

I picked her up and cuddled her to my chest before I laida her on the changing table. I handed her a stuffed elephant and then began to peel off her pajamas and wet diaper. I wanted to dress her in one of the new Christmas outfits I'd bought, but I figured she'd get more of the pancakes on her than in her, so for now I simply pulled on one of her heavy onesies. When she was dressed, I picked her up and went down the stairs. Zak was in the kitchen flipping flapjacks while an old Christmas movie played on the small television above the brick fireplace that had been built into the far wall of the gourmet cooking area.

"Da," Catherine screamed, reaching for him.

Zak handed me the spatula and I handed him the baby.

"How's my little princess this morning?" Zak asked, kissing her on her cheek, which made her giggle.

Catherine pointed to the plate of pancakes. "Eat."

"Yes, we're going to eat," Zak confirmed. "I'm going to let Mommy get you settled in your high chair while I finish up here."

Zak passed Catherine back to me and I put her into her seat. "Where are the girls?" I asked.

"They're still upstairs. I asked them if they wanted pancakes, but they're going to eat later. I have a feeling Shawna watches her calories."

"I guess when you're in the public eye the way she is, watching calories is something you do," I replied.

"Grab the syrup and I'll get the bacon," Zak suggested. "Do you want powdered sugar?"

"No, just syrup is fine. It smells good in here. And not just the pancakes."

Zak nodded to the counter, where I noticed two candles burning. "Pine and bayberry. I picked them up the other day, then forgot about them. They make the whole room smell good."

I smiled as I poured myself a second cup of coffee. "I really love the vanilla candles you put out in the den, but these are nice as well. I was thinking about replacing the stick candles on the mantel in the living room with something that gives off a scent. Maybe cinnamon."

"Speaking of the mantel, I was thinking of replacing the nails we use every year to hang our Christmas stockings with hooks."

"That might be a sturdier option. I'm glad you brought it up; I should get a stocking for Shawna. I'd hate for her not to be able to join in with the family on Christmas morning."

"Do you want me to top off your coffee?" Zak asked, holding up the pot.

"Yes, please." We'd just settled into the booth surrounding the table in our little kitchen nook when a news brief interrupted the movie that had been playing in the background. "What the what?" I said when the woman on the screen informed us that Shawna Jennings had reportedly been abducted from a party in Nashville.

Zak frowned. "Maybe it's a publicity stunt."

I slid out of the booth. "Perhaps. But I think we should find out what's going on."

I left the kitchen and went up the stairs. When I entered Alex's room, I found the girls listening to music. "There's something I think you should see," I said and turned on the television.

"What's going on?" Shawna asked. "Why's my mother on television?"

"According to the news report, you were abducted from a party in Nashville. This isn't some sort of publicity stunt, is it?"

Shawna paled as her own image flashed on the screen. "No," she gasped. "It's not a stunt. The girl at the party pretending to be me is my cousin Amber."

"She looks exactly like you," Alex said.

Shawna nodded. "She does look a lot like me. Especially when she's trying to look like me. She must have found out I was going to go off the grid for a while and took advantage of it to pretend to be me to get into parties I hate but she loves." Shawna frowned as she looked at the screen. "But why would someone want to kidnap me? And who?"

"I don't know," I said, "but we're going to find out."

Shawna stared at the screen. "And why is my mom pretending that I've been abducted? Not a lot of people can tell Amber and me apart when she does her hair and makeup like me, but Mom sure can. Why is she standing there on television telling the world her baby has been taken and she needs their help to get her back?"

"Maybe you should call her," I suggested.

Shawna nodded.

I looked at Alex. "Maybe you both should come downstairs so we can sort this out."

"Yeah, okay," Alex said. "We'll be right down."

Alex came down right away and Shawna joined us after she'd spoken to her mother. As it turned out,

Shawna's mother had realized the girl who'd been taken was Amber and not Shawna and had told the Nashville detective she'd spoken to as much. She'd been frantic to get hold of Shawna, but as part of her peace-and-quiet plot, she'd turned off her cell phone. The Nashville PD had thought it best not to alert the public or, more importantly, the kidnappers, that they'd nabbed the wrong girl. The kidnappers were surely after a ransom and might kill Amber if they realized the girl they were holding wasn't the one who was worth millions of dollars. Shawna's mother and the detective were waiting to get the security footage of the party; all they had so far was a video of Amber being pulled into a black truck outside where the party was held and eyewitness accounts that she'd been there and then taken.

"This is all my fault," Shawna said, running her hands through her hair. "If I hadn't run away from home, Amber would never have gone to that party and would be safe at home."

"It's not your fault," I said. "You didn't make Amber go to that party. You couldn't have known what would happen."

Shawna let out a groan before plopping down in a chair. "Maybe not, but I still feel responsible. Whoever took Amber did it because they thought they were taking me. I told my mom to pay the ransom as soon as the kidnappers make their demand. Whatever they want. All I care about is getting Amber back safely."

"Zak's calling the police," I said. "He'll make your decision to pay the ransom known. I'm sure they'll want to speak to you. Are you and Amber close?"

Shawna shook her head. "Not really. I guess we were when we were younger, but once I turned professional and got better and better known, it seemed like she resented me. We don't hang out anymore, but Amber has faked being me to get into parties in the past. I probably should have made more of a thing about it, but I figured her partying on my reputation didn't really hurt anyone. And," Shawna added, "she was really in to it, while I wasn't."

"You told her you were going to be out of town?" I asked.

Shawna shook her head. "No, but my mom might have mentioned it to her or her mother. I can totally see my mom complaining to them about her ungrateful daughter who canceled a tour to spend the holiday with her mostly absentee father. She was pretty mad when I insisted I wasn't going to spend Christmas in a bunch of hotel rooms and on stages again."

"Does your mom know Amber sometimes pretends to be you?" Alex asked.

"No," Shawna answered. "I don't think so. She wouldn't like it. She'd be afraid Amber would do something to tarnish my reputation. She's very concerned about how I'm perceived, and my fans' opinion of me. She doesn't even want me to leave the house without wearing full makeup. It's exhausting, but that isn't what matters now." Shawna took a deep breath. "I sure hope Amber's okay."

"Do you have any idea who might have kidnapped her?" I asked.

Shawna looked confused and shook her head. "No. I've never been threatened, and I don't think I have any enemies. It must just be someone looking for a big payday."

We all looked up as Zak walked into the room.

"Well?" I asked.

"Shawna's mother is working with the Nashville police, and they seem to have a strategy. I asked if there was anything we could do, but they don't want us to do anything at all right now. They want Shawna to stay here with us. The detective I spoke to feels it's extremely important to the eventual negotiations with the kidnappers that they not know they have the wrong girl."

"So there hasn't been a ransom demand yet?" I verified.

"Not so far. All they have is a video of Amber being pulled into a black truck outside a party where she was known to have been. They assume the demand will be forthcoming. In the meantime, Shawna is to hang low."

"My dad," Shawna said. "We need to tell my dad. If he's heard about the kidnapping he'll be frantic."

Zak's lips tightened. "The detective seemed to be against you doing that, but I agree. He needs to know you're okay. I'll set up a secure line and we can contact him."

I decided to call Ellie while Zak worked with Shawna to set up a line to her father. It seemed apparent we weren't going to make it to the hospital to see her and the baby this morning as we'd planned. Hopefully we'd be able to stop by later in the day.

"Any news?" I asked Alex after getting off the phone.

"Shawna's in the office with Zak. They're doing a conference call with both her parents. I'm not sure how it's going. I heard some raised voices, so I'm staying well out of it."

"Smart girl." I took Catherine out of her high chair and set her on the floor. She squealed with delight when Charlie came over and sat down next to her. "I feel so bad for Shawna. I know she feels responsible, but she really isn't. The poor thing. All she wanted was a few weeks to relax and she couldn't even manage that."

"I bet half the teenage girls in this country would kill to trade places with Shawna—maybe in the whole world—but she doesn't live all that glamorous a life. She works hard," Alex said with passion. "Really hard. And her parents are constantly pulling her in opposite directions. I think she feels that by making a choice about the way she wants to live her life, she's actually making a choice between her parents. It must be awful to feel that way."

I blew out a breath. "Yeah. But I'm sure worrying about her cousin has to be the worst. I hope they find Amber soon and she's okay."

I sat down on the sofa and Alex sat down beside me. She put her head on my shoulder and I stroked her hair as she poured out her heart to me.

"I just don't understand how anyone could do such a thing. Shawna is such a great person. She's sweet and giving and really cares about the people around her. Who would want to kidnap her? People only care about money. It isn't right."

"I know how awful this feels, sweetie. Sometimes life isn't right. But Shawna is safe with us and I'm sure the police will find Amber."

"Do you think whoever has her will hurt her?"

"No," I answered. "I don't think they will. Not if they just want money, which Shawna has already said she's willing to pay."

"What if they don't want money? What if they want something else?"

I sighed. "All we can do is wait and see if the kidnappers send a ransom demand. If Amber was taken last night, I'd think the demand will come through soon." Actually, I was sort of surprised the kidnappers hadn't already made their demands known. Maybe they had. Maybe Zak and Shawna were working out the details for Amber's release right now.

"What's happening?" I asked Zak when he returned to the living area from his office.

"Shawna's mother has received a ransom demand. The kidnapper wants a million dollars wired to an offshore bank account. It's a reasonable amount given Shawna's assets, but her mom is saying no way."

"But it's Shawna's money and she wants to pay the ransom," Alex said.

"That's true. But she doesn't have anywhere near that amount of money in her checking account, and her savings and investment accounts are held jointly with her mother, which means her mother's signature is required to access any of it. It makes sense that the accounts would have been set up that way when they were opened. Shawna was a minor then, and her mother probably was right to want to make sure she didn't waste the money on shopping and whatnot. Shawna just turned eighteen a few weeks ago and the accounts haven't been changed yet. Shawna will need her mother's permission to use the money, and if she can't get that, she'll need a court order to get to it. It doesn't seem as if either of those conditions can be met today."

"But that's not fair," Alex spat. "It's Shawna's money. Her mom should do what she wants."

Zak sat down next to Alex and put his arm around her. "I know, honey. But Shawna's mom seems to have her mind made up. Shawna is still talking to her, but I'm not sure how much good it will do."

"Then we need to give her the money," Alex insisted. "I know you have it, and Shawna will pay you back."

"If it comes down to that, of course I'll lend Shawna the money, but I think for the sake of her relationship with her mother it's best to allow her to at least try to work it out on her own. In the meantime, the police are going to send the security tapes from the party for Shawna to look at. It seems something on the tapes is behind her mother's sudden unwillingness to cooperate. I left while they were still talking. I'm not sure exactly what Shawna's mother saw."

This was one of those times when being a mom was the hardest job in the world. I could see Alex was unhappy and extremely concerned for her friend, but I didn't think there was a thing I could do for either of them. While I wanted to find empathy in my heart for Shawna's mother, I was having a hard time understanding why she would block Shawna's desire to pay the ransom. If the choice were mine, I'd choose people over money any day.

"So what's going on?" Alex asked Shawna when she returned to the living room.

"My mom wants me to watch the video from the party. After that, I'm supposed to call the detective she's working with."

"We'll stream it on the big-screen television in the den," Zak said.

"Yeah," Alex said, giving Shawna a hug. "We'll watch it with you. We all want to help."

"Thanks. I could use the support and the extra sets of eyes. If we can figure out who has Amber, maybe we can get her back."

When it arrived, we settled on the sofa while Zak set up the video feed. He keyed it up, turned it on, and watched the events unfold. The party had taken place at a club that had been reserved for a private gathering. In the beginning, there were only a few people milling around, but as time passed more partygoers began to arrive. Zak handed Shawna the remote control so she could pause the feed, or move it forward or back as she chose.

"Is that Deandrea Wellington?" Alex gasped as a well-endowed blonde flashed onto the screen.

"Yes, that's Andi. She probably came with Carlton Donaldson," Shawna dropped the name of one of the biggest country singers in the business.

"Don't tell me they're dating," Alex gasped.

I almost chuckled out loud as my very intellectual daughter demonstrated she was just as likely to become starstruck as anyone else.

"For a while now," Shawnna confirmed. "You'll see a lot of big names at this party, and a good percentage of them will be doing silly things, but remember, this was a private party where they can be themselves and let their hair down without their fans looking on. Anything we see on this tape should be kept in the strictest confidence."

"Of course," Alex promised her friend. "I totally understand, and you can count on me to keep everyone's secrets under lock and key."

After watching the feed for a few minutes, I began to wonder if allowing Alex to watch the tape with us had been the best idea. I wasn't sure what I was expecting, but apparently those in the music industry were prone to getting wild and crazy when they were out of the spotlight. I don't consider myself to be a prude, but I had to admit I was shocked by some of the antics that flashed across the screen.

"It looks like a lively group," I said after witnessing two of the women tear off their tops before hitting the dance floor.

"Yeah, sorry," Shawna said. "I guess you can see why I never go to these parties. I much prefer staying home with my cat, who loves to cuddle with me while I read by the fire."

"You have a cat?" I asked.

"I do, and he can be as ornery as they come, but I love him. He's staying with my mom while I'm away. If I'd known your house was pet central, I would have brought him."

"Next time for sure," I offered. Then I gasped audibly when a man came through the party riding on a llama.

Shawna laughed. "Not all Nashville parties are this wild. It just so happens Amber picked one of the crazier groups to hang out with."

"Who's that?" Alex asked when a man in black jeans and a black dress shirt flashed across the screen. "He looks familiar."

Shawna's face hardened. "Damn it, Amber, what did you do?"

Chapter 6

I looked at Shawna, who seemed angry rather than frightened. "What is it? What did you see?"

"The guy in the black jeans, Conway Tisdale, is an ex of mine who Amber has always been infatuated with."

"You think they hooked up?" I asked, trying to determine why Shawna was so upset.

"I hope all they did was hook up." Shawna scowled at the screen as Amber walked across the room and melted into Conway's arms.

"What do you mean, that's all you hope they did?" I asked.

Shawna's face was beginning to turn red. "When I first met Conway, I was really drawn to him. He had a way about him that was fun and refreshing. But after we dated for a while, I realized his devil-may-care attitude was really just irresponsibility. When I broke up with him, he stole one of my credit cards and charged over twenty thousand dollars' worth of travel, dining, and electronics before I realized what had happened."

"Wow. Not cool," Alex said.

"Not cool at all," Shawna agreed. "The worst thing about it was that when I confronted him, he just laughed and said I owed him the twenty grand plus a lot more because hanging out with him had helped advance my career. He acted like he should get a cut of my income, like some frigging agent. I told him in no uncertain terms he'd never get another penny from me, and I'd made the right decision when I kicked his sorry backside to the curb."

I frowned when Conway pulled Amber into a hallway that must not have had cameras because they faded from the screen. "Why would Amber be hanging out with a guy like that?"

"Amber thought I deserved what I got from Conway. She made a comment that indicated as much. She didn't think I treated him the way he deserved and called me a self-involved elitist who wouldn't miss the twenty grand and needed to get over myself."

Yikes, this cousin sounded like a real piece of work. I returned my attention to the screen. I watched as Amber returned from the hallway on her own. "I wonder where Conway went." I said when he didn't reappear.

Shawna bit her lip. "I'm beginning to understand why my mom didn't want to pay the ransom and insisted I watch the tape."

"You think she doesn't want to pay the ransom because Amber is hanging out with the man who stole money from you?" Alex said.

"I think she doesn't want to pay the ransom because Amber's hanging out with the man who's most likely trying to steal from me again."

"So you think Conway is the kidnapper?" Zak asked.

Shawna let out a long sigh. "I'm guessing Conway and Amber are in on it together."

I found it hard to believe Amber would do such a thing to her cousin.

"Look there." Alex pointed at the screen.

Amber was walking to the door. We still hadn't seen any sign of Conway since the hallway. Amber glanced around the room and stepped out of the club.

"Now what?" Alex asked.

"Let's just keep watching," Shawna said.

A few minutes after Amber left, Conway came running in, grabbing hold of people and speaking frantically. The video continued to run for quite a while before the police showed up.

"The police are supposed to have another video of Amber being pulled into the black truck," Zak reminded us.

Alex looked at Shawna. "What are you going to do?"

"There's a better than average chance this 'kidnapping' is just a plot cooked up by Amber and Conway to bilk me of a million dollars, but I'm not a hundred percent sure. I don't see how I can do nothing in case I'm wrong and Amber really is in trouble."

"If we can track her down, you'll know one way or another," Zak said.

"How do we do that?" Shawna asked.

"You can see the truck in the video but not the license number. We know where Amber was abducted from. When I have that other video, I'll try to track the truck from that location. If I run it through some of my software, I might be able to enhance things enough to get a partial plate or even a visual of the driver."

Shawna agreed and went into Zak's office to call her mother to ask the police for the other video, and Zak headed into the computer room. I had a feeling the conversation Shawna was about to have wouldn't be pleasant, so I suggested to Alex that she and I and Catherine go into the kitchen to put a snack together. It looked as if we were in for another long day.

"Do you think Shawna's right, and her cousin is part of the plot? I don't understand how she could be so mean," Alex said.

I placed Catherine in her high chair and opened the refrigerator to pull out fruit and cheese. I handed Catherine a few slices of the cheese before I spoke. "We don't know for certain she's done anything. At least not yet. All we know is that she was with someone Shawna doesn't like or trust. That doesn't necessarily make her guilty of anything."

"Shawna thinks she's guilty. I can tell. She said she was only fifty percent sure, but I saw the look of hurt and betrayal on her face when she was watching the video."

I set one jar of olives and another of pickles on the counter next to the cheese. "I noticed that as well. I'm sure this is very hard for her. People who are related don't necessarily get along, but I'd still hope family members wouldn't go out of their way to hurt one another. Can you grab one of the big Christmas platters? Actually, make it two. We'll put the cheese and fruit on one of them, and the meat, olives, and pickles on the other. I'll get some small paper plates and we'll set everything out buffet style so it will be easy to eat."

Alex went to the cabinet to grab the platters. "When I was watching the video it occurred to me that while Amber looks an awful lot like Shawna, she doesn't act like her at all. Do you think the people at the party realized she wasn't Shawna?"

"That's a good question. The people closest to Shawna would be able to see that things weren't quite as they seemed, but we don't know whether Shawna was close to anyone who was at the party."

Alex rolled up the sleeves of her fuzzy Christmas sweater. "It doesn't seem like her sort of crowd. That's what made it the perfect place to stage the kidnapping. There were plenty of people who could testify to what went on, but no one who was paying all that much attention to Amber." Alex began slicing more cheese. "I'm having a hard time figuring out what I'm hoping for."

"What do you mean?"

"I guess I hope Amber wasn't kidnapped, that she faked the whole thing. That would mean she's safe. But I think it's going to hurt Shawna deeply if Amber's trying to steal a million dollars from her."

I opened the jar of pickles and began slicing them. "I think this is going to be hard on Shawna no matter how it turns out. All we can do is be there for her and offer our support when we can."

"Do we still have any garlic spread from the other day?" Alex asked.

"I think there's some left. Maybe we should set it out with some crackers."

"I'll grab them and another plate," Alex offered. "I know Shawna was trying to lose a few pounds— not that she needs to; she's already so thin—but even if she needs to lose the weight to fit into costumes or whatever, if there was ever a time for stress eating, this would be it."

I smiled. "I totally agree. In fact, let's set out a tray with sweets too."

"Do you feel a cold breeze?" Alex asked as I took out cookies and another tray.

I paused. "I do feel cold air coming from somewhere." I looked toward the door to the stairs leading down to the basement. "It feels like there's a draft coming from the basement."

"I'll check," Alex said. "Maybe the gasman left the outside door open."

"The gasman?" I asked.

Alex popped an olive into her mouth and nodded. "When you were out yesterday a man from the gas company came by. He needed to check a possible leak in the system. He asked if you and Zak where home and I told him you weren't, but he said a leak could be dangerous, so he was going to need to take a look around outside. I thought it would be fine, and a gas leak really can be very dangerous. He didn't ask to come in, just said he might need to check the line where it came into the house, so I left the basement door unlocked just in case he needed to get in. Shawna and I were up in my room listening to music and I was afraid I wouldn't hear him if he knocked on the door."

I narrowed my eyes. "What time did he come by?"

Alex shrugged. "I don't remember exactly. It was in the morning, not long after you and Zak left. Is everything okay? I didn't think you'd care if he was on the property to fix a leak."

"Everything's fine," I reassured Alex. "Did you happen to notice if he came inside the house at all?"

Alex's smile faded. "I didn't see him. He said he might need to go into the basement, but he didn't say anything about the rest of the house. If he'd wanted to look around inside the house, I would have called you, but it seemed like he was mostly interested in the line outside." Alex bit her lip. "You seem worried. Should I not have let him look around at all?"

"Was he wearing a uniform from the gas company?" I asked.

Alex nodded. "He had on a uniform and he was driving a gas company truck. I didn't have any reason to think there was something going on other than maybe a gas leak." Alex gasped. "You don't think he was really a paparazzo trying to get confirmation that Shawna was here?"

I shook my head. "I don't think anyone knows she's here. I'm sure he really was just checking on a leak. Why don't you run down and close and lock the door? I'll start taking these things out to the living room."

After I brought the food out and put it on the living room table, I took Catherine upstairs for a nap. It was a little early compared to her usual nap time, but she'd been rubbing her eyes and I think she was picking up on the tension in the room. A nice long nap seemed the better option for her now.

"Da," Catherine said after I set her on the changing table.

"Daddy's working." I handed her a stuffed toy. "Maybe he'll have time to play with you after your nap."

"Lele."

I turned around and watched as Charlie curled up on the rug next to the crib. It could very well be that he was picking up on the tension too.

"Looks like Charlie needs a nap too. He can stay in here with you, but you need to go to sleep, not play with him." I'd leave the door open a crack so he could leave on his own if he changed his mind.

"Dat." Catherine pointed to the stuffed reindeer Zak had bought her when we were in town a few days ago.

I picked it up and handed it to her. "Do you want to sleep with Rudolph today?"

Catherine hugged it to her chest as I picked her up and placed her gently in the crib. I tucked her blanket around her, kissed her forehead, and tiptoed out of the room, pulling the door partially closed behind me. I stopped off in my bedroom to grab the baby monitor I'd left on my nightstand, then headed down the stairs. When I arrived at the bottom of the stairs, Nona was just coming out of her bedroom.

"Are you just getting up?" I asked.

"Late night."

"It's eleven thirty."

Nona grinned. "Like I said, late night. Is the baby down for her nap?"

I nodded. "Just so you know, there's a bit of excitement going on this morning." I filled her in on what had been happening.

"Oh my. That's a shame. Is Shawna all right?"

I tilted my head. "I'm impressed by the way she seems to be holding things together, but obviously she's upset. Zak is trying to help her track down her cousin, and Alex and I made a snack for everyone. It's just deli and crackers. If you want something more substantial, I can make it for you."

"Coffee is fine for now. I'm supposed to meet my guy friend in town for lunch at one."

"Didn't you just come home after being gone for two days?"

Nona shrugged.

"Do you need a ride?" I asked.

She shook her head. "He's picking me up. I think we might take in a show later in the day. In fact, I wouldn't worry if I don't make it home until tomorrow, or even the day after that."

I smiled and rolled my eyes. Nona had become somewhat withdrawn after her stroke. I was happy to see she seemed to have gotten her groove back, but I worried about the way she hooked up with random guys she met in bars. Still, she was an adult and entitled to make her own choices.

Nona continued down the hallway and I went into the room I sometimes used as an office and called the gas company. It was Sunday, so the business office was closed. The woman I spoke to didn't know whether there really had been a gas leak the previous day and suggested I call back in the morning.

"Zak found the truck," Alex said when I returned to the command room, which was really just the living room.

"He found the truck? How?"

"Traffic cams led to a partial plate, which he applied to his filter, and after a bit, he came up with an address."

"Where?"

"A couple of miles from the club. Zak's on the phone with the Nashville police. They're checking it out. Hopefully, that's where Amber is, and we can put this whole thing behind us."

"Shawna?"

"In the office with Zak. She's a wreck, but she's shown real strength."

I had to smile at the fact that words like that had come out of the mouth of a fifteen-year-old. Of course, Alex wasn't your average fifteen-year-old.

After a few minutes Shawna and Zak joined us in the living room. "So?" I asked.

Zak sat down next to me and put an arm around me. "They found the truck in the garage, just as I'd predicted. Amber's jacket was inside, but there was no one in the house. A neighbor verified that Conway Tisdale owned the truck and had been staying in the house, which is owned by a friend of his, who's currently away. Tisdale also owns a red Corvette. We figure Conway and Amber made off in that. The police are looking for it." Zak squeezed my shoulder. "Don't worry, we'll find her."

I looked at Shawna. "So if Amber is with Conway, that must mean she's behind her own kidnapping, just as you suspected."

Shawna bowed her head. The poor thing looked so defeated. "It looks like it. I still can't believe she'd do this to me, but I can't ignore the evidence."

"Is there any chance Conway kidnapped Amber when he ran into her at the party, but she wasn't in it?" I asked.

Shawna's expression grew thoughtful. "I suppose it's possible. Of course, Conway would know she was Amber and not me, but he'd also probably believe I'd pay the ransom to get her back. He has a real grudge against me. I'm sure he thinks a million bucks is just a drop in the bucket compared to what I really owe him."

"Why does he think he helped you with your career?" Alex asked.

"When I met Conway, he was an up-and-comer in the movies. He'd just appeared in a box-office hit and was about to do another one. I was making my name in country music, but he was Hollywood. I was sixteen and he was twenty-four, but we started dating with my mother's blessing. We were together for about six months, and we were seen together a lot. I suppose being with him did provide me with a certain level of publicity. It was after I broke up with him that my career actually took off, but his started to slide. He got into drugs and landed in rehab. He isn't close to being as popular as he was two years ago now. I have no doubt he thinks he deserves payback. I just hope if Amber isn't in on the plan, he doesn't hurt her."

"Do you think he might?" I asked.

Shawna frowned. "I don't know."

Zak phone buzzed. "Zimmerman," he answered. I watched his face as he nodded. "Okay, thanks."

He looked at Shawna. "They got them."

Shawna blew out a breath. "Is Amber okay?"

"She seems to be."

"Was she in on it?"

"They're still sorting it out. Why don't you call you parents? They must be frantic. I'll see if I can get some additional details."

Chapter 7

Tuesday, December 18

After the excitement of Amber's faked kidnapping, life settled down a bit. Shawna had experienced a few dark moments when she'd been provided with the somber news that not only had Amber been in on the kidnapping but the ploy to bilk money from her cousin had been her idea all along. Still, Shawna was determined not to let Amber's actions ruin what was left of her holiday. She seemed to find solace in throwing herself into the Santa's Sleigh project, which was good for everyone.

We still didn't know who had killed Zarek Woodson, but Zak and I met with Salinger to go over the suspect list he'd developed, and while there were a handful of individuals with reasons to want to see an end to the resort idea, we couldn't think of anyone who'd actually want to kill him.

I'd spoken to Scooter several times, and he was having a wonderful time with his father, so for the moment at least it seemed the Zimmerman family was on an even keel. Tuesday was a beautiful sunny day despite the recent snow, so Zak and I took the family dogs for a long walk while Alex and Shawna entertained Catherine.

"Charlie looks like he's getting tired," Zak commented before bending down and scooping the little dog into his arms.

I smiled as Charlie offered Zak a thank-you lick. "It's hard for him to keep up with the bigger dogs when the snow is so deep, even though we've made a track with the snowmobile," I said. "I'm sure he appreciates getting a ride from his daddy."

"Maybe we should pull him on a sled."

I laughed. "He might like that, although when I walk with Catherine, I stick to the paved road. Even if there's a thin layer of snow, the sand stroller works just fine with its bigger wheels. It's easier for Charlie too, although now that I think of it, one of those two-seat strollers would work well for both my little darlings."

Zak smiled. "A double stroller is a good idea. Did you find the one you wanted to buy for Levi and Ellie?"

"I did. It arrived yesterday. Maybe you can put it together and we can drop it off this evening when we bring over their dinner."

"It's nice of you to offer to cook for them all week."

I slid Zak a sideways glance. "We both know that while I made the offer, you've been the one doing all the cooking, but I know they appreciate the effort. Levi has managed to get more volunteers to help out at the tree lot, but he's still there part of every day, and poor Ellie is exhausted."

"Levi said your mom and dad went by and spent a good part of yesterday helping Ellie while we were at the tree lot with Levi."

I nodded. "Ellie has been getting a lot of help. Jeremy told me that Jessica volunteered to take Eli for the day so Ellie could get some sleep."

"Did Jeremy say if he, Jessica, and the kids are joining us for Christmas dinner?"

"They are. Which means we'll have a full house, although I'm a little sad Pi won't be with us this year." Pi had been another of Zak's wards when he was a teenager. He was now a college graduate and was currently overseas working on a project for Zimmerman Software.

"I'm sure he'd come home for the holiday if he wasn't so busy," Zak said. "I'm really proud of him. He's completely taken ownership of the project we're trying to get off the ground. It's very intricate; quite frankly, I wouldn't have attempted it without his help."

"He does have your same knack for technology. Which is great. And I understand it might not be convenient for him to come home from Europe right now. But I'm going to miss him, though we'll have lots of people here. If Phyllis and Ethan come, which I think they will, we'll have twenty-two, although two of them are too young to sit at the table."

"Twenty-three with Shawna," Zak pointed out.

"That's right; I forgot to include her in my count. She seems to be enjoying working on Santa's Sleigh. Alex said she got a bunch of her country music friends to make donations, which means the project can be expanded next year. Alex is even talking about opening a community kitchen during the summer months, when the homeless population down in the valley comes up the mountain to camp."

"The community church already does that on a limited basis. Maybe Alex can piggyback on what's there and they can expand. By the way, I wanted to let you know I got all our donation checks sent out, but I wasn't sure how you wanted to handle the disaster aid group that decided not to allow individuals who were evacuated to bring their pets to the shelter. I know that's a sore point for you."

"It is, and there are plenty of organizations that do allow pets that would welcome the donation. We can go over the list. I had a few new groups I wanted to add this year. Did Phyllis tell you that Ethan decided to get involved with the search-and-rescue team?"

Zak and I turned for home as we continued to discuss our town, our friends, our charities, and our family. Life was good. Sometimes things happened to cast a shadow over that goodness, but overall, our life was exactly the way I dreamed it would be.

******

Later that morning, Zak and I drove into town to pick up a few ingredients for the casserole he was planning for that night's Denton family dinner. The streets were packed with holiday shoppers gathering the last items they needed before the big holiday. I

96

wanted a few more stocking stuffers for the kids, so we parked in the community lot so that we could peruse the shops on Main Street before heading to the market.

"I'm really excited about Christmas this year, but I wonder if we shouldn't be doing more for Catherine's first birthday on Saturday," I said to Zak as I slid my hand into his.

"She's only a year old. I'm not sure how much she'll appreciate a big celebration. I think she'll enjoy a trip into town followed by a family dinner with your parents and Harper just fine."

"I'm sure she will, and I know we talked about keeping it simple, but now I'm thinking we should have invited Levi and Ellie and their kids, and Jeremy and Jessica and their three children. I'm not even a hundred percent sure my mom mentioned it to my grandpa and Hazel. I know it's hard with Catherine's birthday so close to Christmas, but I don't want it to get lost in the holiday."

"If you want to have a larger party, let's have a larger party. We'll still need to do it in the evening, with your mom busy all day with Hometown Christmas, but I don't see why we can't invite the Dentons and the Fishers. We probably should have invited them in the first place. And we definitely need to make sure we've invited your grandfather." Zak glanced into the distance. "The library is open, so why don't we swing over there and talk to Hazel? After that, we can stop by the tree lot to talk to Levi."

I grinned. "Okay, great. I'll call Jeremy after I reconfirm the time with my mom. I'm thinking six. I know that's late for the little ones, but as you said, Mom will be at Hometown Christmas that whole day." I looked across the street at the bakery. "Maybe we should just order a cake. You'll have the meal to worry about and Ellie won't be back to her full strength for a while, so I don't want to ask her to bake it. A bakery cake would be easier."

"I agree. And we'll keep the dinner menu simple as well. Let's order the cake and then go to the library. I'm thinking maybe a princess cake."

I shook my head. "She loves *Bubble Guppies*, so I'm thinking we should do an underwater theme."

"*Bubble Guppies* it is."

We ordered the cake, then set off for the library. I kept thinking Hazel would retire at some point, but she loved her job, and when I spoke to her about it last, she'd made it clear she planned to stay until someone kicked her out. I suppose I could understand her unwillingness to leave behind such an important part of her identity. She'd worked at the library for longer than I'd been alive, and retiring would probably feel a bit like severing a limb.

"Zak; Zoe," Hazel greeted us. "Is Catherine not with you today?"

"She's at home with Alex so Zak and I could get some shopping done. We were at the bakery ordering the cake for Catherine's birthday, and it occurred to me that I wasn't sure my mom mentioned the small party we are having for Catherine on Saturday."

"She hasn't said anything, but we'd love to come. I have story time here at the library as part of the Hometown Christmas event until three."

"Mom will be tied up all day too, so we're thinking of doing a dinner. We'll probably eat around six, but you and Grandpa can come by at around five if you want."

"I can't believe Catherine is already going to be a year old. Time really does fly."

I nodded. "It really does." I glanced at Zak. "We need to run if we're going to get everything done before we have to make the dinner we're taking over to Levi and Ellie this evening."

"How's Ellie doing? I've been meaning to stop by to see her and the baby."

"She's good. Tired but good. Things will be easier once Levi is finished with the tree lot. He's lined up more volunteers, but he's still spending more time than he'd like selling trees."

"I guess you heard about the incident at the lot last evening."

"Incident? I hadn't heard. What happened?"

"The woman Zarek Woodson had been dating just before he died walked onto the lot and basically attacked a man who was there with his family. From what I heard, it was quite the stir. Levi had gone for the day and one of the dads from the football team was keeping an eye on things. Not a good situation."

"Olivia Wilson attacked someone?" I asked, referring to Zarek's current lady friend. "Who? And why?"

"Seems to me the man was at the party last week. I'm sorry, his name escapes me. Salinger would know. As for why, from what people overheard, it seemed Ms. Wilson was convinced he was the one who killed Zarek." Hazel glanced toward the front door just as two teenage girls walked into the library. "Everything I know I learned second hand."

"Thanks, Hazel. We'll head over to the sheriff's office now."

We chatted with Hazel for a few more minutes, then headed back out onto the crowded sidewalk. The throngs were so thick by this point that I couldn't see more than a person or two in front of me. Zak took my hand and I let him lead me where we needed to go. He was almost a foot and a half taller than me and so much more capable of negotiating the crowd.

"Olivia Wilson doesn't seem like the type to get involved in a physical altercation," I commented. "Not that I know her well, but she always struck me as being so prissy." I paused. "I guess that sounds mean, and I didn't intend it that way. It's just that I can't see her putting herself in a situation where she might break a nail or mess up her hair."

"The man she'd been dating was just murdered," Zak said gently.

"True. Her emotions might have been running high. I wonder who she attacked. When I think of the men who were at the party, not a single one comes to mind as a possibility. Maybe the guy from Philadelphia who'd been planning a move to Ashton Falls? What was his name?"

"Roland Small?"

"That's right. He's sort of an odd guy. He came to the party with a beautiful woman whose name I can't recall, but his eyes took in every other female in the room. To be honest, there was one moment when I seriously almost decked him."

Zak chuckled. "First an attack at the Christmas tree lot and now we're talking about a fistfight at a political cocktail party."

I playfully punched Zak in the arm. "I didn't actually hit anyone. Seriously, though, men need to learn to keep their creepy eyes to themselves.

Remember that guy with the toupee that looked like he had a cat on top of his head we met in Denver a few years ago? Talk about a scumbag."

Zak stopped walking. I wasn't paying all that much attention and almost ran into a woman who was walking past me. "What is it?"

"It's not a *what* but a *who*."

"Okay, who do you see?" I tried to find what Zak was looking at, but the crowd was too dense.

"Alisha Cobalter."

I shrugged. "So? She was at the cocktail party, and we knew she planned to stay in town until after the first of the year. She can be a real pain in the butt, but I don't think we need to worry about her. We aren't doing any more construction or remodeling that might land us in hot water."

"But the fact that she's in town isn't what caught my eye. What I find interesting is that she's talking to Garrison Ford." Garrison Ford, the owner of Bear Mountain, the largest ski resort in the area.

"I suppose that while Garrison and Alisha usually have very little in common and are known to butt heads, Zarek's project would have provided them with some common ground. At least temporarily. Now that the new resort is most likely dead in the water, they can start staring daggers at each other again."

"I don't expect that to be happening anytime soon." Zak grinned.

I raised a brow. "I can't see over this crowd to know what you're looking at. Perhaps you should give me a bit more information."

"It would appear they may be on a date. They're walking on the lake side of the street, casually looking at the shop windows, but more intently looking at each other."

"Alisha and Garrison?" I frowned. "That doesn't make sense. The two of them are at each other's throats most of the time."

Zak shrugged. "As we said, Zarek and his project provided them with a shared enemy. Maybe having an opportunity to work together provided just what they needed to realize they had even more in common than they thought."

A ski area owner and an avid environmentalist? No, that could never be. Could it? "Should we cross over and say hi?" I wondered.

"No. Let's just continue on to Salinger's office. Whether the two are a couple isn't our business, and they look as if they don't want to be disturbed."

When we arrived at the sheriff's office, we found the reception area empty. The front door was open, so I assumed someone was around and headed down the hall. Salinger was in his office, but he was on the phone. He held up a finger and I indicated we'd wait for him in the conference room. I wasn't sure who he was on the phone with or whether he cared if he was overheard.

"Sorry about that," Salinger said when he joined us.

"No problem," I answered. "We didn't want to disturb you."

"New receptionist. That woman pops out for a smoke at least a few times a day. I'm going to have to talk to her again about leaving the place unattended. So, how can I help you today?"

"We were in town running some errands and stopped to see Hazel. She gave us the news about

Olivia Wilson attacking someone at the tree lot last night."

"Carson Amundson. Ms. Wilson apparently is convinced Amundson was the one who killed Zarek. She attacked him while he was helping his niece and nephew pick out a tree."

"Was anyone hurt?" Zak asked.

Salinger shook his head. "Not really. Amundson has some fairly deep scratches on his face, but nothing critical."

"Did you arrest Olivia?" I asked.

"No. She was drunk and obviously highly emotional about Zarek's death. Amundson didn't want to press charges, so I drove her home and told her to sober up. I'd say she's nursing a hell of a hangover today."

"Did she tell you why she thought Carson was the one who killed Zarek?" I asked.

"She said something about backstabbing, betrayed trust, and broken promises. I didn't catch it all; to tell you the truth, she wasn't making a lot of sense. But hey, she was totally wasted. I thought I might try to follow up with her after she's had the chance to sober up a bit."

"There was something odd going on with Carson at the party," I said. "He greeted everyone at the front door and then disappeared."

"I guess that is a little odd." Salinger frowned. "Maybe once I'm able to have a real conversation with Ms. Wilson this will start to make sense."

"Have you had any other breaks in the case?" I asked.

"Not really," Salinger admitted. "I've been working on the suspect list I came up with. I've managed to talk to all five owners of the existing ski areas, as well as several of the more vocal members of Alisha Cobalter's group. I haven't been able track her down yet, but maybe she'll finally return my call today."

"So no one stands out as possibly being the killer?" Zak asked.

Salinger shook his head. "I still have a few folks to follow up with, and there are still three men who were at the party that I need to try to get more information out of. I keep thinking something will pop, but so far this investigation is going very slowly."

"Who do you still need to speak to from the guests at the party?" Zak asked.

"Lake Wildman, Byron Coleman, and Jasper Quinan. I don't suppose you know anything about any of them?"

"A bit. Coleman is from out of town," Zak informed Salinger. "I think his main residence is in Boston, but he has a place in Washington, DC, as well. He's a serious investor who's connected politically here and internationally. He's known to be ruthless and uses those connections to his advantage. He seems to be willing to take risks, which is probably why Zarek invited him to the meet and greet. I don't know Coleman well, but I can't see that he'd have a reason to want Zarek dead. Now, the senator is another thing altogether. I understand Coleman and he have gone head-to-head on a number of occasions over legislation that affects investors."

"So why would he come to a party in the senator's honor if he didn't get along with him?" I asked.

"I suspect he was spying."

"Okay, then why did Zarek invite him if he was a spy?"

"Coleman invested quite a bit of money in Zarek's project, so I imagine if he asked him for an invite, he'd comply." Zak looked at Salinger. "You made an offhanded comment about the senator possibly being the actual intended victim. Have you learned anything that might suggest that to be the truth?"

"It's a possibility, though there's no evidence to back it up, so I'm conducting the investigation from the assumption Woodson was the intended victim. If I discover any evidence to the contrary, I'll switch gears. What's your take on Quinan?"

"He's an interesting guy. Unlike most of the other guests, who either inherited their fortunes or made them by means of developing and running successful businesses, Quinan made his by gambling," Zak answered.

Salinger seemed taken aback. "Really?"

Zak nodded. "He made his first couple of million by entering and winning a high-stakes poker tournament. He took that money and entered other tournaments and doubled his cash and then doubled it again. He won twenty million dollars in a state lottery and an additional thirty or forty million on high-risk investments. It's taken him some time, but he won himself quite a little nest egg. Of course, now that he has money to invest, he focuses his time doing only that. Being a gambler, he likes the risky stuff. His motto seems to be 'the bigger the risk, the bigger the reward.' So far, he's managed to keep coming out on top."

"Do you think he had a motive for wanting Woodson dead?" Salinger asked.

Zak paused before answering. "Not that I can think of off the top of my head. I think Quinan was going to invest in the ski resort. He seemed to be on board with the concept and didn't care about the political stuff one way or another. There was something, though."

Salinger leaned in just a bit. "Go on."

"It appeared there might have been something going on between Zarek and Quinan's wife."

"Now that you mention it, I agree," I joined in the conversation. "There was definitely an underlying vibe between the two."

Salinger pulled out a pad and a pen and made a note. "'An underlying vibe' seems to be just the kind of thing I should look in to. What about Wildman?"

"Lake's a local who, of the three men we're talking about, probably had the most to gain or lose from Zarek's venture, although I have no idea why he'd be interested in a cocktail party thrown in honor of Senator Goodman," Zak said.

"So you think his presence might have had more to do with the ski resort than Goodman's run for governor?" Salinger asked.

"Perhaps. I wondered about his presence at the party that night and I tried to decide exactly what his role might have been afterward. Unlike most of the people in the room, Lake doesn't have a lot of cash to invest. He does okay for himself, but he's in no way in the same league financially as the other investors there. I spoke to Alton Biswell at the party. I believe he was on your list?"

Salinger nodded. "Yes. I've spoken to and cleared him."

"Alton initially was interested in the project, but when I spoke to him at the party, he indicated he was going to bow out. According to what he told me, the reason he changed his mind was because Zarek was involved in a dispute with his business partners. It had occurred to me, given Lake's presence at the party, he might have been the second business partner Alton referred to. I meant to follow up with him, but I never had the chance."

"If you want to leave his number with me, I'll follow up," Salinger offered. "If Lake Wildman was Woodson's second partner, I think a serious conversation with both him and Amundson might be in order."

Chapter 8

After we left Salinger's office, we headed back toward the shops in search of the additional stocking stuffers I'd decided I needed. I received a text from my mother just as we were leaving the candy store. She needed my help with something and had called the house. Alex had told her Zak and I were in town, and she hoped if we still were nearby, we could stop by the kitchen at the community center. The facility wasn't all that far from where we were, so I texted back to say we were on our way.

"Did she say what the problem was?" Zak asked as we walked past the rink, where kids of all ages were ice-skating to holiday tunes.

"No. She's been having more than her share of problems with the event this year. And the worst thing is that none of them are her fault or could have been prevented. It's almost like Hometown Christmas is cursed."

Zak took my hand in his. "I don't think the event is cursed, but there does seem to have been a lot more glitches than usual. And the event doesn't even start for a few more days. I hope for your mother's sake that things begin to fall into place."

When we arrived at the community center we found my mother pacing back and forth as she talked to someone on the phone. I could see she was more than just a little harassed, but until she got off the phone and explained the situation I couldn't help. After a moment she hung up and looked at me.

"Do you have extra tree lights?" Mom asked.

I glanced at Zak.

"A few," he answered.

"Someone ran into the big tree in the town square with their car. The tree is totally destroyed and the lights and ornaments are broken into a million pieces. I have a photographer from the *Bryton Lake Courier* coming this evening to take publicity photos. He specifically wanted one of the Victorian carolers in front of the tree. I called Levi, and he's bringing over the biggest tree he has left on the lot, but we need lights. The holiday store sold out of tree lights this morning. They offered to order some, but it will take a few days to get them. I could send someone to Bryton Lake, but I don't know if we have time for that before the photographer arrives."

"I have lights," Zak promised. "I'll go get them."

Mom put her hand on his arm. "Thank you, dear."

"And I'll go over to the town square to help Levi with the tree," I offered.

Mom smiled at me.

"Don't worry," I assured the woman who had given me life and finally become part of my world only recently. "We'll have everything looking great before the photographer arrives."

As it turned out, Levi managed to get his football team to cut and transport a huge thirty-foot tree for the town. It was a bit tricky getting it secured, but with the help of the fire department, we got it in place. As soon as it was tightened down, the team got to work on the lights Zak had rounded up. Not only had he brought our spare strings but he got Alex to work calling folks in town and asking them to bring their spare strings to the town square as well. In the end, redecorating the tree turned into a fun and meaningful community event in its own right.

"The tree looks fantastic," I said several hours later as I stepped back to admire our handiwork.

"It really does." Mom sighed. She turned and hugged me. "Thank you so much for jumping in when I needed you. I must be out of practice; this event seems to be getting the best of me."

"It's not your fault everything keeps going wrong. You're doing a wonderful job. There's no way you could have prevented what happened to the first tree. And this tree is great."

"It is."

"Zak and I need to get going. Alex is babysitting and I should relieve her, and Zak and I promised to bring dinner to the Dentons, which reminds me: We've decided to invite Levi, Ellie, and kids, as well as Jeremy, Jessica, and their kids to Catherine's birthday party on Saturday. Grandpa and Hazel too."

"That's a nice idea."

"You'll be tied up with Hometown Christmas during the day, so we're going to do a dinner. I'm thinking we'll eat at around six."

"That should be fine, barring another emergency."

I wanted to reassure my mom that things would go smoothly from this point forward, but with all of the problems she'd been having, I honestly wasn't sure they would.

******

"This looks delicious; thank you so much," Ellie said as she slid the casserole we'd brought into the oven to keep warm.

"How are you feeling today?" I asked as I walked over to the cradle that was set up near the sofa and took a peek at my beautiful goddaughter.

"Better. I'm still tired, but I managed to get a good long nap today after Jessica came to pick up Eli. And your mom helped out yesterday. Everyone has been so great."

"Two babies under two is a real handful. We're all happy to help out. By the way, Zak and I are having a small birthday party for Catherine on Saturday. A dinner. I hope all the Dentons can attend."

"We wouldn't miss it for anything."

"Miss what?" Levi asked as he walked into the room. He must just have gotten home from the tree lot.

I explained about the party. "Thanks for helping out with the replacement tree," I added.

"Replacement tree?" Ellie asked.

"Some guy plowed into the Christmas tree in the town square and totally destroyed it," I said. "Levi found a nice big new one, Zak and Alex rounded up a batch of lights, and practically everyone in town helped to redecorate it in time for the photographer who was coming from Bryton Lake to take pictures of it."

"It wasn't a guy," Levi said.

"What do you mean?"

"You said some guy plowed into the tree. It wasn't a guy. It was Olivia Wilson."

I put a hand to my mouth. "Oh my. I hadn't heard that."

"She was drunk again and tried to run down Carson Amundson, who barely escaped with his life."

"Oh my gosh. That's awful."

"It's awful for everyone. Olivia is going to be spending the holidays in jail and Carson has a huge gash on his arm. Salinger is beating himself up for not arresting her after the incident at the tree lot and everyone feels bad that Olivia is taking Zarek's death so hard."

"She seems certain Carson killed Zarek," Ellie said. "Do you think he did?"

I glanced at Zak, who shrugged.

"I'm not sure," I said at last. "But there definitely was something odd going on with Carson at the cocktail party. He greeted everyone at the door and then disappeared. I never saw him again after everyone arrived. If he was Zarek's business partner, it seems he would have stuck around to help with the guests, although technically it was supposed to be a political event for Senator Goodman."

"Yeah, that's definitely strange," Ellie agreed.

"How long had Olivia been dating Zarek?" Levi asked.

Everyone looked at Zak. "I guess about six months. Maybe not even that long. I ran into Zarek at a fund-raiser this past spring and he was with a woman he'd met overseas. I don't remember her name, but I think she was French. I'm sure Olivia came into the picture after that."

"Does anyone know why Olivia is so certain Carson killed Zarek?" Ellie asked.

"According to Salinger, she said something about backstabbing, betrayed trust, and broken promises, I think," I replied. "That was after the attack at the tree lot, and I didn't pay a lot of attention to her exact words. Now, however, I think a closer look might be warranted."

"We can call Salinger later," Zak said. "I'm sure he'll get to the bottom of whatever happened."

I thought about Carson's odd behavior at the party, and remembered Zak and I had seen him having lunch with Senator Goodman's beautiful publicist the day after his business partner's death. I wondered if Carson might be the one behind that. I hadn't known Carson before I met him at the cocktail party, and Agent Stanwell had said that whoever was behind Zarek's death was most likely known to me. Carson as the killer didn't fit when you took that into account; he wouldn't have known my routine or whether I'd bring my purse with me to the party. But if whoever was behind Zarek's death had slipped the vial into my bag after I arrived in Zarek's home, Carson was one of only two people I could think of who might have done it. Maybe this wasn't just Olivia's unhappy, drunken notion and he was the one responsible after all.

"Other than Carson Amundson, are there any strong suspects?" Levi asked.

"Four that I know of," I answered. "Not that any of them are particularly good suspects, but of all the guests at the party, four others stand out as having the strongest motives. Travis Zukerman was there, despite his zero-growth policy, as was Alisha Cobalter, who, by the way, we saw in town with Garrison Ford."

"Alisha and Garrison?" Ellie asked.

"You wouldn't think they'd have a lot in common, but they both had reason not to want to see Zarek's project become a reality. The only other person Salinger is taking a close look at is a man named Jasper Quinan."

"And why would he want Zarek dead?" Levi asked.

"He might have had something going on with his wife."

"Sounds like a good reason to want a man dead," Levi said.

"So between Carson Amundson, Travis Zukerman, Alisha, Garrison, and this guy Quinan, do you have a front runner at this point?"

I looked at Zak.

"I'd say Carson, based on what we know so far," Zak answered.

"Me too." I nodded.

The conversation moved on to topics other than Ashton Falls' most recent murder. We talked about Catherine's birthday party, and Christmas, and New Year's Eve. It was nice to have plans with friends who felt like family.

"Did I tell you my mom is coming for New Year's?" Ellie asked after a brief lull.

"You didn't say, but I'm not surprised. She does have a new granddaughter I'm sure she'll want to dote on. It'll be nice to see her."

"Yeah." Ellie sighed.

"Am I picking up on a lack of enthusiasm there?" I asked.

"She's bringing Sam."

"The new boyfriend?"

"Not so new," Ellie said. "They've been dating for five months now and living together for two. It's going to be weird to have a man I don't even know sleeping in the guest room with my mother."

I offered Ellie a look of sympathy. "I can see that. Maybe he'll be willing to sleep on the sofa, or maybe your mom and he can get a hotel room."

Ellie shook her head. "I can't ask Mom to go to a hotel, and while I'd like to suggest the sofa for Sam, I'd feel like such a hypocrite. I mean, I lived with Levi for a long time before we were married. Heck, we weren't even dating when I got pregnant with Eli. I'm afraid the whole outraged-daughter thing would make me look like a hypocrite. It's just that…"

"It's just that it's your mother and it feels weird."

"Exactly."

"So talk to her. If you don't, you'll be uncomfortable, and chances are your mom will pick up on it. It might end up being even harder on both of you if you don't at least tell her how you feel before she gets here."

Ellie took a deep breath and blew it out slowly. "I guess you're right. And who knows, maybe she'll be just as uncomfortable as I am."

"Maybe. Other than you not being comfortable with your mom having sex with him in your guest room, what do you think of Sam?"

Ellie shrugged. "I don't really know him. He's a retired airline pilot who gets to travel all over the world for almost nothing. He's already taken Mom to Rome and Paris. They're doing Switzerland and the Scandinavian countries in the spring. I'm sure it will be lovely."

"And your mom seems happy?"

Ellie smiled. "Very. She has an active social life now, and Sam owns a large home in a gated community with pools, a golf course, a club house, and a gym. Mom says she feels twenty years younger. She's lost quite a bit of weight and has taken up yoga. It's like she has a new lease on life, and I'm happy for her. It's just that—"

"She isn't the mom you grew up with."

Ellie laughed. "What are you, a psychic?"

"Maybe not a psychic, but I get it. Your mother was very momish when she lived here. She owned a restaurant, she loved to cook, she played bridge with the girls and volunteered in the community. I don't remember her going on a single trip other than to visit your aunt. And now she has a hot new boyfriend, travels to Europe at the drop of a hat, and does yoga. She has a new life, and you're afraid that new life won't have room in it for her old daughter. Not that I mean you're old," I clarified. "You know what I mean."

"I do know, and you're exactly right. It's like she's a completely different person. A more energetic, happier person, but still a different person.

I wonder if she'll have room in her life for her daughter and grandchildren."

"She'll have room, I promise. This visit will be good for you. It sounds like maybe you need to get reacquainted."

"That sounds like a ridiculous thing to say about your own mother."

"Is it? You know, it was almost as if I had to get to know my mom for the first time when she moved to Ashton Falls. In a way, her transformation was the opposite of your mom's. She went from being a single jet-setter who attended exclusive parties and dined with royalty to being just a mom who's focused on raising her baby and a wife to the man she always loved but never really spent any time with. She went from partying with the elite to chairing a local Christmas event. I had to let go of everything I thought I knew about her to make room for the new woman she'd decided to become." I took Ellie's hand and gave it a squeeze. "And you know what? I'm so glad I did. I love who my mom became, and I think once you get used to the changes, you'll love the new life your mom has embraced as well."

"I guess." Ellie looked less than certain. I hoped this visit went as well as it needed to for both Ellie and her mom to move on to the next chapter in their relationship.

Chapter 9

Wednesday, December 19

Salinger had been busy with Olivia when I'd called the night before, so I told him to get back to me when he had the time. Unfortunately, that opportunity didn't present itself until the following morning, so I'd had to be patient. Waiting patiently wasn't my strong suit, so when Salinger did finally call, Alex volunteered to keep an eye on Catherine so Zak and I could go to Salinger's office right away.

"I spoke to Olivia Wilson after she was arrested, and she made a compelling argument pointing to Carson as the one responsible for Zarek's death," Salinger said after we were seated in his office.

"What sort of argument did she present to even get you to listen to her after the way she's been acting?" I asked.

"Zarek was working closely with both Lake Wildman and Carson Amundson regarding the ski resort early on. She hadn't been dating Zarek when they first hatched the plan, but he shared the details of their conversations after they became a couple. According to Olivia, while all three men developed the idea together, when it came to doing the legwork to get the project off the ground, Lake Wildman faded into the woodwork. Zarek agreed to let him continue to be involved, but he was only a very minor partner because he hadn't pitched in at all when it came time to find investors, apply for permits, draw up plans, etc. She claimed Wildman was fine with his reduced role."

"That fits what I've observed," Zak said. "But how did we get from three friends brainstorming over a beer to Olivia trying to kill Carson?"

"I'm getting to that," Salinger continued. "After Lake took a back seat, Zarek and Carson worked together in a more active manner and seemed to have some success in finding the investors they needed. They were sailing right along until they hit their snag with the local environmentalists. Once folks like Travis Zukerman and Alisha Cobalter got involved to work against them, Zarek and Carson began to part ways in terms of strategy. In Olivia's opinion, Zarek had very definite opinions about the exclusivity of the resort, which was something he'd promised his foreign investors, while Carson felt the project would be dead in the water without local help, which is why he went to Senator Goodman. Goodman felt if the project was ever going to come to fruition, it needed to be reworked so it would appeal to the masses. Carson was willing to look at it as a scaled-back resort, but Zarek wasn't, which led to problems between them."

"I can see how the exclusivity of the resort could be an issue," Zak replied. "Zarek promised his foreign investors a certain type of resort when he pitched the idea to them, but I understand why the senator wouldn't be interested in backing a project that would exclude most of his constituents. While the debate on how to proceed would most likely be a lively one, how would it lead to murder?"

"Olivia said Zarek was adamant the original plan was the one he was going to pursue and refused to make the changes Goodman was asking for, but she later found out that Carson made a backroom deal with Goodman's aide agreeing to the changes he wanted. Olivia knew Carson was never going to convince Zarek to go along with those changes and was crazy to promise Goodman as much, so in her mind, the means by which Carson planned to keep his promise to Goodman was by killing Zarek, eliminating him from the picture."

"But why go to such elaborate means?" I asked. "And why would Zarek throw the meet and greet for Senator Goodman if they weren't seeing eye to eye on the resort?"

"Because Zarek believed if he invited his rich and influential friends to a party in Goodman's honor, the senator would realize he had a lot of power and influence and might give in on the exclusivity issue. I don't know what would have happened if Zarek hadn't died, but now it seems the project is back on within the new parameters."

I sat back and let myself digest that. Things were beginning to make sense, but there were still a whole lot of unanswered questions. "I guess that answers some questions, but why the poison? There had to be an easier and cleaner way to kill someone than to sneak a vial of toxin into a party in the purse of one of the guests. It's too complicated to be considered a good plan."

"I agree," Salinger said. "The whole thing is so bizarre. I don't have a theory that accounts for who killed Zarek or whether his death had to do with his connection with Goodman and his interest in the resort."

"I feel like we're missing something. It's almost as if the bizarreness is the point."

"What do you mean?" Salinger asked.

"The first bizarre thing is that Zarek Woodson died in his own home in front of a roomful of people. Why? I know we've asked this many times in the past few days, but really, *why*? We agree that if you want someone dead, there are easier methods of making that happen. Why come up with something so elaborate in which there are so many moving parts that could get messed up? Why not just shoot the guy or strangle him in his sleep? Carson was his partner and must have had access to him. Why the elaborate show?"

Salinger shrugged.

"And then the second bizarre thing is that a man who may or may not be a legitimate federal agent asks Zak and me to come to his hotel room so he can interview us. Not only is the request strange, but his interviews were too. It was almost like he needed to keep us there for a certain amount of time, so he asked me to go over everything that had happened in agonizing detail, which seemed totally unnecessary to me."

"Zoe's right," Zak said. "The guy did seem to be stalling."

"That does seem odd," Salinger agreed.

"More than odd. Not only did he drag out my interview to an annoying degree, but he slowly and painstakingly examined my purse as well as its contents. I mean, I get it if he thought the purse was the method by which the toxin was brought into the house, but why wouldn't he just confiscate the bag and take it to a lab?"

"Another good point," Salinger said.

My eyes grew big. "Unless he actually was stalling?" I looked at Zak. "When Alex and I were in the kitchen on Sunday while you and Shawna were working on the kidnapping, we felt a cold draft. Alex suggested maybe the gasman had left the basement door open. I asked her what she meant, and she told me a man from the gas company had come by on Saturday shortly after we left to speak to Agent Stanwell. This gasman said he was there to check on a leak, and if he found one, he might need to check where the main line came into the house. Alex knew that was through the basement, so she told him she'd leave the basement door unlocked in case he needed to go in there. She and Shawna were upstairs listening to music, and she was afraid she wouldn't hear if he knocked on the door."

"What are you saying?" Zak asked.

"What if the man wasn't really from the gas company? What if he was there for some other reason and Agent Stanwell dragged the interview out as long as he did to give the guy at the house enough time to do whatever it was he was really there to do?"

"You think he came into your home while you were away?" Salinger asked.

"He might have. If the dogs were upstairs with the girls and he was quiet, he could have come in without alerting anyone. Especially because Alex knew he was on the property to fix a gas leak and wouldn't have been concerned about a minimal amount of noise."

"Do you think he was there to rob you?" Salinger asked.

"Probably not," I said. "But that doesn't mean he wasn't after something."

Zak stood up. "I need to go home to take a look around. Check out the security system. I'm not liking this one bit."

＊＊＊＊＊＊

The rate at which Zak sped toward home most definitely exceeded the speed limit, but I didn't think Salinger or any of his men would give him a ticket. The first thing Zak did was to call the gas company. The person he spoke to confirmed they hadn't had a repairman in our area to fix any leaks on Saturday. It seemed, as we had begun to suspect, Agent Stanwell—or whoever he really was—had been working with a partner. Zak was more than just a little upset, but knowing the man was likely not legit answered a lot of questions for me about the wacky interview I'd been struggling to understand.

"So do you think your purse was used to smuggle in the toxin that killed Zarek after all?" Nona asked when I explained what we'd learned.

"Probably not. There's no doubt Zarek was poisoned, but the person who put the poison in his drink must have been the one who brought it into the cocktail party. I'd say Stanwell somehow knew that and used Zarek's death to get Zak and me out of the house for a couple of hours while his partner did whatever he came here to do."

"It was bad timing I stayed in town and Alex and Shawna were here alone," Nona said.

"It isn't your fault. Shawna is an adult and Alex is almost one. The fact that they were here alone wasn't the problem. The man who showed up was wearing an official-looking uniform and was driving an official-looking truck. Alex isn't to blame for allowing him to look around. I would have done the same thing had I been here."

"What do you think the guy was after?" Nona asked.

"I don't know, but given the sensitive nature of the work Zak does, I have a feeling whatever he was after isn't going to be something as simple as would be stolen in some random burglary."

"Do you think they got into his office or the computer room?"

I shook my head. "Probably not. Zak keeps both locked up good and tight, but if he got into the basement, he might have messed with the cables that run into them. I guess we'll have to wait and see what Zak finds. In the meantime, I'm going to drop Alex and Shawna off at Phyllis's house. They'll be there to work on the food baskets for Santa's Sleigh. After that I'm going into town with Catherine. It's a nice day and I think she'd enjoy a day out. Besides, I'd like to give Zak some space while he tries to figure out what that man was really doing here. Do you want to come?"

"I would, but I have a date."

"Another date? Is there someone special in the picture?"

Nona grinned. "Perhaps. But I'd like to keep my love life to myself for now. If the *someone* special turns into *something* special, I'll be sure to let you know."

After I dropped off Alex and Shawna I headed into town. I hadn't been to Donovan's, the general store my grandpa founded and my dad still owned and operated, since Dad had decorated for Christmas, and I knew Catherine would get a kick out of his mechanical reindeer, so I started there.

"What a nice surprise," my dad said when I walked through the front door with Catherine in my arms.

"Pa." Catherine reached for her grandpa.

"Aren't you just the cutest little Christmas baby?" my dad said as he reached for Catherine, who was dressed in a reindeer sweater and green corduroy pants.

"Dat." Catherine pointed to the display Dad set out each year that included mechanical animals displayed in a forest setting.

"That's Roland the Reindeer," Dad said, carrying Catherine over for a closer look. "He's spending Christmas in the forest with Randy the Raccoon and Roxy the Rabbit."

Catherine grinned.

"Is it okay with Mommy if you have a cookie?"

"Maybe half a cookie," I said.

Dad set Catherine in the high chair he kept on hand for when she visited and gave her half a soft oatmeal cookie. "Does Mommy want a cookie too?"

"Mommy does." I accepted it and took a bite. It tasted like Hazel's recipe. She must have dropped them off. "It's quiet in here today."

"It's just a lull. The guys were here earlier, but they left at lunchtime."

The guys my dad was referring to were my grandpa and his friends, who stopped in most days of the week, sat by the potbellied stove, and played checkers.

"I was hoping to run into Ethan. I want to invite him for Christmas dinner."

"He mentioned he was planning to have dinner at your place. I think Phyllis must have told him about Christmas when she invited him to Catherine's party. Or maybe Zak did. Where is Zak today?"

I explained about the fake repairman and Zak's urgent search for clues to what he'd been after.

"Does Zak think his software has been compromised?"

"He doesn't know yet. Right now it appears someone went to a lot of trouble to do something, so we're assuming it was something big."

Dad frowned. "Do you think whatever was going on at your house was in any way related to Zarek Woodson's death?"

I let out a breath. "I sort of doubt it. I mean, I think the man who interviewed Zak and me and his partner, who dressed up as a gas company repairman, took advantage of the fact that we witnessed Zarek's death to get us out of the house, but I'd be surprised to learn Zarek was killed as a plot to gain access to our house." I took another bite of my cookie. "At this point the whole thing is pretty confusing. We spoke to Salinger this morning and it seems he has the suspect list in Zarek's death narrowed down to five people. Maybe if he can figure out which of the party guests actually killed Zarek, we can figure out if that was related to the arrival of the fake repairman."

"Who does Salinger have it narrowed down to?"

"Travis Zukerman, Alisha Cobalter, Garrison Ford, Carson Amundson, and Jasper Quinan."

"I can't imagine Travis, Alisha, or Garrison would kill anyone. I don't know the other two men well enough to have an opinion about them. I heard Carson Amundson was responsible for the damage to the town tree."

"Carson didn't damage it directly. Zarek's girlfriend, Olivia Wilson, tried to run him over and hit the tree instead. Still, from what I currently know, I'd say he's probably at the top of my suspect list."

"You haven't been investigating?" Dad said in a voice bathed in caution.

I shook my head. "No. Not really. Zak and I have talked to Salinger a few times, but that's the extent of our involvement. I'll admit to being curious, however. Have you heard anything else?"

Dad shrugged. "You know how folks talk. I can't say I've heard anything I'd bother to repeat, although Ethan did say Garrison's lease with the forest service is up for renewal next year, and if Zarek had managed to get the funding for his fancy resort, he could very well have been eligible to compete with the existing ski areas for land use permits."

"That's actually a big deal," I said. "A huge deal. The lease option only comes up about once every quarter of a century. I know Garrison and the other operators own the infrastructure connected to their own resorts, but they lease the land from the forest service. As far as I know, the forest service has never failed to renew a lease when it's come up, but they could if they felt motivated to do it."

"Sure. I'm not saying it would happen, but at this point there are five resorts around the lake, each with their own long-term lease. Theoretically, if a sixth player came on the scene with an offer that would benefit the forest service over what the other resorts are offering, they could decide to give the lease for the land to someone else when it came up for option. A new lease isn't guaranteed; a new contract has to be negotiated with each renewal. I know when Beaver Gorge renewed two years ago, Snow Canyon to their north tried to outbid them in an effort to double the area available to them for ski runs. The forest service ended up making a new deal with Beaver Gorge, but it was touch-and-go for a while there."

"So theoretically, if Zarek had been able to take over Garrison's lease, he could have built his resort on the land currently being leased by Bear Mountain, which would allow him to build his resort without any additional land coverage."

Dad nodded. "In a nutshell."

If the possible loss of a resort you'd spent decades building wasn't motive for murder, I didn't know what would be.

Chapter 10

When Catherine and I left Donovan's we headed to the tree lot to say hi to Levi. Catherine loved all the colorful lights and the sound of "Frosty the Snowman" on the stereo system made her squeal with delight. Levi offered Catherine a tiny set of reindeer ears that she seemed more interested in eating than wearing. He offered me a set as well, which I happily slid onto my head. We chatted for a few minutes, but I could see he was superbusy and didn't really have time to talk. He did say he hoped some additional volunteers would show up because Ellie had been in a blue mood that morning when he left home, and he was feeling bad about not getting home sooner. I would have volunteered to take over at the tree lot for him, but I had Catherine, so instead I offered to pick up some food and drive over to the boathouse to provide Ellie with some company until he could get away. It was a sunny day but still cold, so I picked up soup and garlic bread from Rosie's.

"Thanks so much for coming by," Ellie said with a hug. "For some reason I've been feeling sort of deflated ever since I woke up."

"It's normal to feel that way after having a baby. I can remember feeling sort of blue for weeks after Catherine was born. I can also remember feeling bad about not feeling happier, which made me feel even worse."

Ellie laughed. "It does seem to be a vicious cycle."

"Let's give Catherine and Eli a sandwich and then we can let them play while we enjoy our soup and have a nice chat."

"Sounds perfect." Ellie opened the cupboard and pulled out a loaf of bread. "Did you talk to Salinger this morning? I meant to call you after last night's discussion, but I never got around to it."

"Zak and I did talk to Salinger and it looks like Zarek might not be the only victim around here."

Ellie gasped. "Someone else is dead?"

"Not dead." I told her about the fake repairman and that the man we'd spoken to on Saturday probably wasn't an agent at all, but just a man trying to keep us away from the house.

"Oh no." Ellie cut a sandwich in quarters and gave each baby a piece. "Is anything missing?"

"Zak was frantically trying to figure that out when Catherine and I decided to give him some space. We aren't worried about missing stuff as much as we are about compromised data."

"Zak has a really good security system. I'd think it would be hard for anyone to get in."

"Close to impossible even. But if the guy who interviewed us and the guy who came to the house saying he needed to repair the gas line were working together, it seems they have a fairly organized operation. If the system has been compromised, Zak will fix it. I just hope he can fix it before anything sensitive ends up in the wrong hands."

"Poor Zak," Ellie said. "Poor Alex. I bet she feels horrible."

"She does, though I've tried to reassure her that she didn't do anything I wouldn't have done in her place, but she was almost inconsolable when Phyllis called and invited her and Shawna over. Talk about perfect timing. It gave Zak the peace and quiet he needed and gave Alex a break from the stress of it all."

Ellie poured milk into sippy cups and handed them out. "This has been the oddest week. First Zarek is killed in front of a room full of people, then Shawna's cousin fakes her own kidnapping, and now this. Do you think the breach at your house has anything to do with Zarek's death?"

"I don't know. I just hope nothing critical has been compromised. Alex will never forgive herself."

Eli started calling for another piece of sandwich, although Catherine was still working on her first piece. Ellie got up to give her son what he wanted, while I poured the soup into bowls we could pop into the microwave.

"So, on the subject of Zarek's murder, what have you learned?" Ellie asked.

"Salinger has five suspects. In my mind, the strongest two are Carson Amundson and Garrison Ford."

"Why Garrison?" Ellie asked.

I explained about the lease renewal.

"Wow, that is a good reason for wanting someone out of the way. Do you really think Zarek could have stolen the lease right out from under Garrison?"

I shrugged. "Maybe. Each ski resort has a long-term lease with the forest service to use the land. The resort owners pay for the infrastructure as well as all the maintenance and upgrades, but they don't own the land. In exchange for the right to use that, the resorts negotiate a contract that compensates the forest service in some way. As long as an agreement is reached, the leases are renewed and nothing changes. I suppose if someone came along and offered the forest service a better deal than the one they'd been getting before, there'd be a discussion about it at the very least. Even if Zarek hadn't been able to steal the lease away from Garrison, I could see Garrison ending up having to pay a whole lot more for the use of the land with the new contract. In fact, I bet making sure the forest service gets the best deal they can is the reason for the twenty-five-year-contract limits."

"Didn't you tell me Carson Amundson is still interested in going ahead with the project he'd been working on with Zarek?"

I nodded. "I did say that."

"Then if Garrison killed Zarek to keep him from creating a problem with his forest service contract and I was Carson, I'd most definitely be watching my back."

Ellie had a really good point there. I couldn't picture Garrison as a killer, but he did have a lot to lose, and he was at the cocktail party. If I had to choose a killer right now, I'd probably have to choose him, closely followed by Carson. I didn't see Alisha as the guilty party. She seemed to be able to inflict plenty of pain by tying things up in court for an indefinite period of time if she didn't like what you were doing. And Travis didn't seem to have a specific motive. Sure, he opposed the new resort, but that was a long way off in the future, even with the support of the senator.

I didn't know Jasper Quinan and had no idea if something really had been going on between Zarek and his wife, and even if there had been, I didn't how he felt about it.

By the time I got home, Zak had discovered that some of the cameras for our home security system had been cut in to. What that meant was that any images picked up by those cameras could be seen by whoever had hacked into the system. Fortunately, the part of the system that had been compromised didn't include the cameras inside Zak's office or the computer room. The security system for those rooms worked on a closed loop independent of the one for the rest of the house. Still, it seemed pretty clear someone was watching us. The compromised cameras covered the exterior of the house, the entries, the staircases, and the hallways. We didn't have cameras in any of the bedrooms or suites.

The breach could have been worse and I doubted our voyeur had seen anything of real interest, but the fact that someone had been watching us gave me the creeps.

"I feel like I'm missing something," I said to Zak again after he explained the extent of the security breach. "Why would anyone want to watch us?"

"It's possible the person who spliced into the camera system was after something in my office or computer lab and wasn't aware those rooms aren't part of the larger house system. I've called Salinger, who's on his way over. I'm not sure what he can do that I haven't already done, but it was important to file an official report." Zak glanced at my purse, which I'd tossed on the kitchen counter. "You said the man who identified himself as Agent Stanwell went through your purse."

I nodded. "He took every single item out, examined it, and then replaced it."

Zak got up and crossed the room. He picked up my purse and began emptying the contents onto the kitchen table. I sat quietly, waiting for him to finish. In a minute, he picked up a tiny round object. "Just as I thought. It's a listening device."

"Someone has been listening to us?"

Zak nodded. "I'm going to take a look around. There may be similar devices in the house."

"Alex said she didn't think the man came inside. He told her he was going to be working outside and might need to check the main line going into the basement, which is why she left the basement door from the outside of the house unlocked."

"If she was upstairs and the door from the basement to the kitchen wasn't locked, he may have found a way to plant a few devices without her knowing it." Zak picked up my phone. He logged into my settings app. "It looks like someone has been tracking your phone as well."

"The guy did spend a lot of time going through my phone. I was watching the whole time, but he was talking to me and asking questions, and I guess I got distracted a time or two. Damn, I should have thought to check the phone before this."

"Before this you had no reason to think your phone may have been tampered with."

I let out a sigh. "Yeah, I guess not." The fact that someone had been watching and listening to us left me feeling vulnerable. The fact that someone had been tracking my moves left me terrified. I glanced at Catherine and realized if I was in danger, there was a good chance she was too.

"I need to pick up the girls from Phyllis's," I said.

"I'll call Phyllis and ask her if she can drop them off here," Zak offered. "Why don't you take Catherine up to bed? When Salinger gets here we'll figure out what to do."

I nodded. "Okay. I'm going to give Catherine a bath, but I won't be long." I glanced at the dogs, who were watching my every move. "I think the dogs might need to go out."

"I'll take them," Zak said.

******

"My men are dusting for prints, although I doubt we'll find any," Salinger informed us when he arrived with two deputies. "Do you believe the breach has been contained?"

Zak nodded. "I swept the house for bugs. The place is clean. The only phone that was tracked was Zoe's, and I deactivated that option and added a new layer of security. Any luck with the security cameras at the hotel?"

"The guy who interviewed you arrived just before you did. He left after the interviews and hasn't been back. I spoke to the manager, who was able to verify that the man rented a room for the night but didn't show up with any luggage. We still haven't been able to find out his real name."

"Do you mind if I take a look at the tapes?" Zak asked.

"I'll have a copy sent to you. What about the man who was pretending to be from the gas company? Did your cameras catch his image?"

Zak nodded. "I reviewed the tapes from Saturday morning. A truck with an official logo from the gas company came through the gate at nine twenty. A man with a medium build and dark hair wearing a gas company uniform is seen heading to the front door. He wore a baseball cap that partially masked his face, but I was able to observe him speak to Alex at the door and then walk around to the side of the house after she shut it again. Shortly after that, the cameras went offline. The rest of the security system was offline before that, so no alarm would have been triggered. It appears the cameras were offline for about twenty minutes. When they came back on, the man and the truck were gone."

"Did you get a good enough image to identify the guy?" Salinger said.

"He did a good job of keeping his head down, but I managed to get one pretty good shot of him. I'm running it through my facial recognition program. It could take a while, but given enough time I'm sure I'll get him."

"Any idea what they were after?" Salinger asked.

Zak sighed. "I don't know. If I had to guess, he was after something in my office or perhaps the coding to the new software program I'm working on with Pi. The program, once complete, will be worth billions of dollars. Of course, there's no way I'd risk a breach at that level, and I'd be willing to bet the man who was here would know that even if he had managed to infiltrate the computer room, he'd never have been able to hack into the system files, which probably have more security attached to them than the computer files at the White House. No, I'd say he was after something accessible. Maybe files relating to a Zimmerman Academy student or staff person. Or perhaps financial records he hoped to use to access my bank and investment accounts. If Alex hadn't been here, he might have been able to get into my office. On the other hand, if Alex hadn't been here, the alarm system would have been on and he never would have made it onto the grounds, let alone into the house."

I entered the conversation I'd only been listening to up to this point. "Something about this scenario doesn't fit. If there's someone out there who planned to steal something from Zak, whether it was computer code or files, why did the man who identified himself as Agent Stanwell allow us to see his face? And why would he rent a room in such a public place to conduct the interviews? Why wouldn't he wait until we left the estate for another reason, like a trip to town, to show up with the gas company ruse?"

"I suppose it's possible the man who was pretending to be from the gas company showed up here to watch us, not to take anything from us, but if that's the case, I'm even more freaked out than I would be if I could confirm the theft of a file or a code was the real reason for him being here," Zak said slowly.

I found I agreed with him.

Chapter 11

Saturday, December 22

Shawna had donned a black wig and dark sunglasses so she could join the family for Hometown Christmas. At first I wasn't sure the disguise would work, but now, with her signature blond hair covered, she really did look like a different girl. Scooter had returned home late the night before, and Levi had found coverage for the tree lot for the weekend, so the entire Denton family was planning to meet the Zimmermans at the ice-skating rink when it opened at eleven a.m. From there we'd explore the town, eat junk food, visit Santa, and experience all Hometown Christmas had to offer.

At least that was the plan.

"What do you mean, Santa is in the hospital?" I asked my mom.

"I mean the man who was supposed to dress up as Santa and sit in the Santa House today had a heart attack late last night. It sounds like he's going to be all right, but certainly not in time to play Santa this weekend. Your grandpa said he'd do it, but he was supposed to watch Harper for me while I'm busy supervising and your dad's running the kiddie carnival. Can she hang out with you guys?"

"Of course. Harper is welcome to hang out with us any time. You know that."

"I do, but I also know you have your hands full right now, which is why I didn't ask you in the first place."

I looked around. "Where is she?"

"She's over at the church auditorium where the kids are getting fitted for their costumes for the Christmas play tomorrow. Your grandpa is there with her now, but if you could go over to relieve him, that would be very helpful."

I hugged my mom. "I'm on my way. And relax. Everything's going to be fine. And even if it isn't, it'll all be over by Monday."

Mom groaned as she walked away.

I told Zak what I was doing and arranged to meet the group in the food court once I'd collected Harper. Catherine and Eli were riding in the double stroller we'd bought for Levi and Ellie and Levi was carrying Alya in a front pack. The baby was so bundled up you couldn't even see her, but I was willing to bet she was happy and warm curled up next to her daddy's heartbeat.

I was halfway to the church when I spotted someone I'd thought I'd never see again: Agent Stanwell. I realize logic would dictate I'd call Salinger immediately and then wait for him to arrive to confront the man, but logic was never my strong suit, which is how I ended up changing direction and making a beeline for him, despite not having any idea what I'd do once I caught up with him.

"Agent Stanwell," I called after him as he rounded a corner and momentarily disappeared from sight.

When I rounded the corner he was waiting for me to catch up with him. "Ms. Zimmerman. What can I do for you today?"

"You can tell me why you've been spying on me," I answered in a voice much too loud for a very busy and very public sidewalk.

Agent Stanwell placed his hand on my arm. "Perhaps we should take this conversation somewhere else."

I pulled my arm away. "I'm not going anywhere with you."

He looked around at the throngs of people on the sidewalk. "Do you really think this is the best place for this conversation?"

Perhaps he had a point. "There's a bar on the corner. It isn't open yet, but I know the owner. I'm sure he'll let us sit in one of the booths while he's getting things ready."

Agent Stanwell followed the direction of my gaze. "Lead the way and I'll follow."

Damn it, Zoe, I thought to myself. Zak was going to kill me when he found out I'd confronted the man he'd been looking for without at least calling for backup first. Though I'd suggested we talk in a public place and he'd been fine with that, so it was probably all right to assume he wasn't going to kill me.

"Hey, Zeke," I said to the man who owned the bar and was restocking the alcohol supply behind the bar when we walked in.

"Zoe. How's it going?"

"Good. Listen, I need to speak to Agent Stanwell here, and we'd like a bit more privacy than we'd find outside among the crowd. Would it be okay if we sat in one of your booths for a few minutes?"

Zeke nodded. "Fine by me. I still need to sweep up in here, but you can use the big booth in the back."

"Thanks. We shouldn't be long." I led Stanwell to the back of the bar. As soon as we slid into the booth, I pulled out my phone. "I need to call my husband. I was on my way to pick up my sister at the church. I need to let him know I'll be delayed."

"Very well. In fact, ask him to meet us here if he can. I may as well speak to you both at the same time."

"If there's someone else who can pick up my sister, I'll ask him to join us."

He sat back and waited for me to make my call.

"Hey," I said when Zak answered. "I was on my way to pick up Harper when I ran into Agent Stanwell."

"Are you okay?" His voice was tense.

"I'm fine. He wants to talk to both of us. We're in the bar on the corner of Main and Pine. Do you think you can ask Alex and Shawna to pick up Harper, and maybe Levi and Ellie can watch Catherine for a few minutes? I don't think this will take long."

"Don't move. I'm on my way."

I hung up and then turned to the man. "He's on his way."

"I assume, given that you're all in a huff, that you found the bug I placed in your purse?"

I nodded. "Zak found it and that you've been tracking my phone, and that some guy pretending to be a gas repairman, who we suspect is working with you, spliced into some cameras in our security system at the house. Why?"

"Don't you think we should wait for your husband?"

I glanced at the door. I figured Zak would be here in a few minutes, so as curious as I was to hear what this guy had to say for himself, it wouldn't hurt to wait. It was less than two minutes before Zak stormed through the door with Salinger on his heels.

"No need for the gun," Agent Stanwell said to Salinger, who held his gun in his hand.

"Identify yourself," Salinger said.

I saw Zeke pause and watch the drama unfold before him. Looked like he'd have a juicy piece of gossip to share with his customers later today.

"My name is Clarence Stanwell. I work for Senator Goodman."

Salinger frowned. "Senator Goodman?"

He nodded. "I'm a member of his private security team. If you'll holster that gun and join us, I'll explain everything."

Zak glanced at me. I shrugged. Zak slid into the booth next to me. Salinger hesitated, then asked the man for identification. He slowly slid his hand into his pocket and pulled out his ID. Salinger looked it over, then put his gun into his holster and pulled a chair up to the end of the booth.

"Okay, we're all here. Why were you spying on us?" I demanded.

"We had reason to believe the drink that led to Zarek Woodson's death was intended for Senator Goodman. We also suspected one of you," Stanwell looked from Zak to me, "were responsible for the toxin being added to the drink."

"What?" I asked, barely able to contain myself. "Why would you think that?"

"The senator has been getting a lot of hate mail lately, and several very threatening emails demanding he not only abandon his plan to seek the governorship but to give up his seat in the Senate and leave political life behind. The senator was unwilling to cave in to those threats. The company I work for was hired to discover the source of the threats and to protect the senator. Given the threats, we decided to dig into Mr. Woodson's death on the chance the poison was really meant for the senator. In the course of speaking to witnesses, it was revealed that your husband," Stanwell glanced at Zak again, "had reason to want the senator out of the way and might very well be the one behind both Woodson's death and the threatening emails the senator had been receiving."

"That's ridiculous," Zak spat. "Why would I want to kill anyone?"

Stanwell directed his reply to Zak. "Now that I've completed my investigation, I don't believe you're the person we're after. When I interviewed both you and your wife, however, we had conflicting reports and weren't sure who to believe. We decided to watch you and then decide what to do with the intel we gathered."

"Intel?" I asked. "What intel? Why would anyone say Zak had a reason for wanting Senator Goodman dead?"

He leaned forward slightly and placed his hands on the table in front of him, his fingers knitted together. "Didn't you tell me you were at a party in the senator's honor even though you didn't support his run for governor or agree with his political views?"

"Well, yeah," I admitted. "But it's a pretty big leap from disagreeing with someone's politics to killing them."

"Not as big a leap as you might think, but we had more." Stanwell looked at Zak again. "Is it true the software company you own is currently developing a state-of-the-art communications system for Rosso Enterprises, an Italian company owned by Ivan Popov, a man of Russian descent?"

"Well, yes. But that has nothing to do with politics. Rosso Enterprises is a private firm that hired my company to develop a specific piece of software."

Stanwell's eyes narrowed on Zak. "Did you know that Senator Goodman has taken a hard stance in relation to proposed legislation to limit such dealings? It is, in fact, his opinion that American companies should be forbidden from developing advanced technology with a potential for military applications for foreign companies, even when a military application isn't at the root of the technology at the time of development."

"I know there are politicians who feel technological advancements of any type should be kept within the United States, but Zimmerman Software is an international firm, and this particular piece of software is being developed outside the United States. The project is headed by an associate of mine out of the Italian division of Zimmerman Software."

I knew Zak was referring to Pi, who'd been in Italy for months.

Stanwell leaned in slightly. "I've spent the last week looking into your company, your politics, and your finances. At this point I believe we were misled by the information initially provided to us, and we no longer consider you a suspect in either Woodson's death or the threats on Goodman's life."

Zak frowned. "Who provided you with the false intel?"

"Byron Coleman. We believe, after looking into the matter, that Mr. Coleman is responsible for Mr. Woodson's death, the threats against the senator, and the wild-goose chase we've been engaged in this week."

"Why would Coleman want to kill the senator and pin it on Zak?" I asked.

"The disagreements between Coleman and the senator go way back. There are any number of reasons why Coleman might want the senator out of the way. As for why he tried to pin Woodson's death on your husband, I believe it was strictly a financial move."

"Financial?"

"Mr. Coleman has invested heavily in Aquinas Technology."

"Ah," Zak said.

"Ah?" I asked. "Ah what?"

"Aquinas Technology is Rosso Enterprises' main competitor. If the software my associate and I are developing does what we hope it will, it's likely to set Aquinas Technology back quite a bit."

I turned back to Stanwell. "I guess I understand why you did what you did, but it was still illegal and pretty uncool."

"Perhaps," Stanwell admitted. "I suppose we could have just taken the false information we were fed and used it to arrest your husband and sort it out afterward."

I glanced at Zak.

"It's okay," he said. He looked Stanwell in the eye. "Salinger is going to confirm everything you've just told us, and providing you aren't lying again, we'll let bygones be bygones. I've disabled all the surveillance measures you put into place in my home and on my wife's phone and beefed up security in general. I can assure you, another breach is unlikely to ever occur. If you should have further questions about my actions at any time, just ask."

Stanwell laughed. "Will do. And just to be clear, I personally didn't think you'd done what Coleman accused you of once I had the chance to speak to you. I was, however, under orders to find proof of your involvement in Woodson's death and the threats to the senator, which is where the surveillance came in."

"Understood."

Zak might understand, but I was still pretty mad. In the spirit of getting back to the Christmas season, though, I decided to let it go.

Stanwell agreed to go back to Salinger's office with him so he could go over everything he had just told us.

I slid out of the booth. "Just to confirm what I believe you said," I said before he walked away, "do you have reason to believe Coleman killed Zarek in a failed attempt to kill Senator Goodman?"

"Yes. We do have reason to believe that."

I paused to consider this scenario. Zak and I had been talking to both Senator Goodman and Zarek Woodson when Zarek started to gasp for air. There had been a table nearby where both the senator and Zarek had set down their drinks while they shook hands and schmoozed potential supporters. I could see how they could mix up their drinks, but I wasn't sure when and how Coleman could have poured the poison into the drink. I seemed to remember he'd shown up late and then kept his distance. At no point did I remember him approaching the area where Zarek and Goodman were holding court. In fact, it seemed he'd intentionally kept in the shadows, as if to observe without being drawn into conversation. I supposed he might have found a way to get the toxin into the drink without my having noticed. "And Coleman?" I asked. "Where is he now?"

"In the wind, but we'll get him."

"And the senator?" I asked.

"Safely back in DC, where I suspect he'll stay until we catch up with Coleman."

"If you were hired to protect Senator Goodman and he's in Washington, why are you still here?" I wondered.

"I'm leaving this afternoon. I just had one thing to finish up first. I'm glad I had a chance to explain things to you, though. After I met you and realized the intel we were fed was probably fake, I felt bad about the way things went down."

I wanted to tell him there were no hard feelings, but there were still plenty of hard feelings on my part.

"Do you buy everything he said?" I asked Zak after Stanwell left with Salinger.

"I do, actually. What he said made perfect sense, and if there's any doubt, we'll find out when Salinger checks in with the senator to confirm his story. I'm sorry Zarek was caught in the middle of things."

"If Coleman was angry enough about your project to try to frame you for a death it appears he's responsible for, do you think he, or someone else with money to lose, will try again?"

Zak took my hand in his and led me to the door. "I honestly don't know. What I do changes the world. It opens some doors and closes others. I suppose for every fortune I help to make, there could be another fortune my software helps to destroy. I don't mean to sound cold. It certainly isn't intentional or malicious. But change is inevitable, and with it often comes a transfer of both wealth and power."

I paused, considering Zak. "Does it bother you that a victory for Zimmerman Software can correspond to a failure for someone else?"

"Sometimes, but I've found the most radical change occurs in a culture of competition. Without competition, I'm not sure the world would have seen the advancements in science, technology, and even medicine it has."

I supposed Zak had a point. But I hated the fact that for there to be winners, there also seemed to have to be losers.

Chapter 12

"I'm glad we decided to do this," Zak said as we sat side by side watching Catherine open her birthday presents. At least she was opening her presents in theory. In reality she was much more interested in the bows and wrapping paper than anything else, and her Aunt Harper was helping to keep things moving along by doing a lot of the actual work during those times when Catherine became distracted from the task at hand.

"Me too." I snapped yet another photo. "When Catherine finishes with her presents I think we'll do the cake. I have a feeling she might not make it all that much longer, and I want to be sure we have the chance to sing to her before I take her up to bed."

"It's been a long day between Hometown Christmas and the party," Zak said. "I'm surprised she hasn't already curled up on the floor with her blanket and a stuffed animal and gone to sleep."

I glanced at Eli, who'd done just that. The poor little guy. Catherine had taken a nap in the stroller earlier in the day, but Eli had been so fascinated by everything that had been going on around him that he hadn't nodded off at all then.

"I think we're going to go," Levi said, sitting down next to me. "Eli has crashed and Ellie is exhausted."

"I understand," I said. "I'm going to do the cake next, but if you don't want to wait, I'll save you some."

"To be honest, after an entire day of eating junk food, I'm sugared out, and the others probably are too. But thanks for the offer. It's an adorable cake."

"Are you going to the children's play tomorrow?" I asked.

"We plan to if Ellie and the kids aren't too tired."

I kissed Levi on the cheek. "We'll text you tomorrow. Zak is making pulled pork tacos if you guys want to come by. We're thinking early, maybe around four."

"Are you making your famous margaritas as well?"

I nodded. "That's the plan."

"Sounds awesome. I'll check with Ellie and let you know."

Shortly after the Dentons had gone everyone who was left sang "Happy Birthday" to Catherine, Jeremy and his family left, and I took Catherine up to bed. By the time I got my tired little birthday girl tucked in and returned downstairs, Alex, Scooter, Shawna, and Harper had retired to the den to watch *It's a Very Merry Muppets Christmas Movie*, and Zak had opened a couple of bottles of wine to share with my mother, father, grandfather, and Hazel. I poured my own glass of wine and sat down on the sofa next to Zak.

"So what are we talking about?" I asked.

"I was just catching everyone up on Zarek's murder investigation," Zak said.

"How very tragic if Zarek died as the result of drinking a poison meant for someone else," Mom said.

"I think it's pretty tragic whatever way you look at it," Dad said.

"Well, yeah," Mom acknowledged, "but somehow it seems worse if he died in someone else's stead. Are you sure that's what happened?"

I shook my head. "Not really. It's the opinion of the man from Senator Goodman's security team that Goodman was the intended victim, but he didn't have any proof to support it, and the more I think about it, the less I see how Coleman could have been the one to taint the drink."

"Why do you say that?" Grandpa asked.

"Zarek and Senator Goodman were standing at a table near the center of the room so they could mingle. Folks came by to meet the senator and chat for a while. Both Zarek and the senator had drinks they'd placed on a table, but neither was doing a lot of drinking. A waiter was working the room, picking up empty glasses and handing out fresh drinks. There was also a bar manned by a bartender who was making drinks to order." I paused briefly to think about what I remembered. "Coleman came to the party late and seemed to hang back along the far wall, where several men who didn't live in town had congregated. Zak and I planned to leave early, but we didn't want to duck out without at least saying hi to Zarek and the senator, so I was watching them for an opening. I remember the waiter coming around and leaving fresh drinks for them, even though they hadn't finished the ones they already had. Shortly after that, the couple the senator had been talking to stepped away, and I took advantage of the lull to walk over and say hello before anyone else got to them first. As Zak and I went toward them, I noticed Zarek take a sip of his drink. He set it back down on the table to shake Zak's hand and take care of the introductions. It was while we were chatting with them that Zarek began to struggle for breathe. He was dead just a few minutes later."

"So it must have been the sip he took from the fresh drink that did him in," Grandpa said.

"That would be my guess." I looked at Zak. "If the drink came from the bar, and I think it must have, the toxin had to have been added to it either by the bartender, the waiter, or someone who was standing at the bar when the drink was made. Coleman was all the way across the room. I'm sure of it."

"Zoe's right," Zak said. "Coleman didn't approach the bar after he came in. He went over to talk to the men chatting with Lake Wildman. I don't even remember whether he was drinking. If he was, it must have been something brought to him by the waiter."

"So who was near the bar when the drinks delivered to Zarek and the senator were made?" Hazel asked.

"I'm not sure," I said. "I wasn't paying all that much attention, but I bet Salinger has the surveillance footage from the party. Maybe we can figure out who was nearby and could have slipped the toxin into the drink." I looked at the group. "I'm going to call him."

As it turned out, there wasn't a surveillance video of the cocktail party, but when Salinger had been chatting with him earlier in the afternoon, Stanwell had provided copies of photographs he'd collected during his investigation. Apparently, one of the guests, who'd been there as a plus one, was a reporter who'd been stealthily snapping photos the entire evening. Salinger offered to bring the photos to the house so Zak and I could look at them.

"The photos aren't time-stamped, so it's hard to put them in order," I said. "But the couple speaking to Zarek and the senator in this photo is the one I was watching before we stepped up to speak to them," I said.

"The angle is wrong to see who's at the bar," Zak said.

"But maybe we can splice together an overall view of the room with all the photos we have." I picked up the stack and began to sort them. "The group behind and to the left of the senator consists of Garrison Ford, Alisha Cobalter, the man from Aspen whose name I can't remember and his wife, and someone to the wife's left who was wearing a blue suit."

"Here's the same group from a different angle," Zak said. "The man in the blue suit came with Garrison. I think he's a friend of his from out of town. I'm not sure knowing his name is important, but while the man from Aspen and his wife are cut off in this photo, we can see the group standing to the left of the man in the blue suit."

"Jasper Quinan and someone I don't recognize," Salinger said.

"My idea is to piece these together like a puzzle. The photos won't fit perfectly, but maybe if we take clues from each photo, it will help us to find others from the same period in time." I set the first photo with Zarek, Senator Goodman, and the couple they'd been talking to in the center of the table. Then I set the photo with Garrison, Alisha, and the man from Aspen in close proximity of the first one, which would most likely have been taken soon before or after. I set down the photo of Jasper Quinan and the man he was talking to. We eliminated a bunch of others we determined must have been taken before the photo we were using as a base and continued to place others we identified as possible clues on the table depending on who was standing next to whom. Eventually, we had a very rough picture of the period when Zarek and Senator Goodman were chatting with the couple before we approached them.

"The drinks on the table in the base photo are half gone, so I assume the new drinks hadn't yet been brought over to them," Zak said.

"The couple the men were talking to left right after the drinks were delivered," I said firmly. "This photo of the bar shows the bartender chatting with a woman wearing a black dress. We can only see her back. And there's a man in a black suit who I think might be the guy from Denver who was there with Travis Zukerman and another man."

"All we can see of him is his elbow."

"Probably Zukerman," I said. "Who's the guy in the reflection?"

Zak took a closer look at the photo. There was a man standing behind the bar, but far enough from the bartender not to be part of the photo. He was close enough, however, that a portion of his reflection showed in the mirror behind the bar. "I think that's Carson Amundson," Zak said.

I frowned. "I don't remember seeing him at the party after he greeted everyone."

"There's a doorway behind the bar that leads to a storage area," Zak said. "When I went to get our drinks when we first arrived, I asked the bartender if he had Midleton Irish Whiskey. He said there wasn't any under the bar, but he had some in the back and offered to get me a glass. The door looks like part of the wall. I suppose if Carson was around he could have slipped into the room through the doorway. Very few people would have noticed."

"I was focused on the senator as I waited for an opening to approach him, not looking at the bar," I admitted.

"Olivia Wilson has been saying all along that it was Carson who poisoned Zarek," Salinger said. "Maybe I should bring him in for another chat." Salinger pointed to the photo. "Do you know who the woman in the black dress is?"

"I'm not sure," I said. "Most of the women in the room were wearing black dresses, including me."

"Maybe if Travis is the man whose elbow we see, he'll know who the woman was," I suggested. I looked at Salinger. "Have you spoken to the bartender?"

"I have," Salinger said. "It seems whiskey sours were being circulated around the room. That's the senator's favorite drink. Anyone who wanted something else could go over to the bar and the bartender would make it for them."

"There was also a table with wine," I added.

"It appears both the senator and Zarek were drinking the whiskey sours the bartender was pouring en masse," Zak said.

"Which makes sense if it was the senator's favorite. You know, now that I think about it, the drinks that were being carried around on trays might have been poured in the back." I glanced at the photo of the bar again. "In this photo, which must have been taken within a few minutes of the tainted drink being delivered to Zarek, the bartender is just chatting with the people standing near him. He isn't busy pouring drinks for the trays."

"It does make sense that the drinks the waiter took around were made somewhere other than the bar," Zak agreed.

I looked at Salinger. "Have you interviewed the waiter?"

"No. I tried to track him down, but no one admits knowing his name. The bartender said he was already on the premises when he arrived."

"Do we have a photo of the waiter?" I asked.

Zak, Salinger, and I all sorted through the remaining photos. The reporter might have been taking photos on the sly, but he sure had taken a lot of them. They weren't of good quality, so I imagined he must have used his phone to take them when he thought no one was looking.

"Here's one," Zak said, holding it up. "See, the guy's in the background."

I took a closer look at the photo. "Now that I'm focusing on the guy, I feel like I might know him from somewhere." I glanced at Zak. "Does he look familiar to you?"

Zak shook his head. "I don't think so."

"I wasn't paying a bit of attention to him while we were at the party. I was more focused on doing the socially acceptable minimum required before we could get the heck out of there without seeming rude." I picked up the photo and took a closer look. "He seems familiar, but for the life of me, I can't place him."

"Maybe it'll come to you," Salinger said.

"Yeah. Maybe."

"So, back to the overall picture," Salinger directed. "Do you think this collage adequately represents the room in the moments before Zarek was poisoned?"

I took another look. "Yes, I'd say these photos represent the guest dispersal prior to the tainted drink being delivered. The couple speaking to Zarek and the senator were at the table for ten or fifteen minutes. I headed straight to them after the man and woman walked away. The tainted drink hadn't been delivered yet, so it's possible some of the folks in this series of photos moved before it was, but I think this gives us a general picture of who was doing what in the moments leading up to Zarek's death."

Salinger took out his phone and took a photo of the spread on the table. I suggested we tape them together for future reference. While I did that, Zak called Travis to find out if he had indeed been the man at the bar whose elbow we could make out but whose identity we couldn't. He said he hadn't been at the bar before Zarek's death; rather, he'd been in the far-right corner of the room with several men who were in Ashton Falls to consider Zarek's resort project. We dug through the photos again until we were able to verify that, indeed, Travis had been where he said he was.

"I need to have another conversation with the bartender and track down the waiter," Salinger said. "I'll do both tomorrow."

"Let us know what you find out," I said. "The family will be in town for a good part of the afternoon, but we'll be here in the morning, and I'll have my cell with me all day."

"And see if you can find out who the woman at the bar is," Zak said. "There's something about her that's tickling a memory at the back of my mind."

Chapter 13

Sunday, December 23

"Dat," Catherine said, pointing to the stage.

I hugged the curly-haired baby on my lap. "That's Harper. Isn't she cute in her little lamb costume?"

Catherine grinned and clapped her hands together.

"When you get older you can be a lambie in the play too."

Catherine turned to Eli, who was sitting on Levi's lap to my right. She grabbed his arm and pointed at the stage. "Dat."

Eli grinned. "Doggy."

"Actually, that's supposed to be a donkey," Levi corrected.

"I can't wait for Eli to be old enough to be in the play," Ellie commented. I could tell she was missing Alya, who was being cared for by Jeremy's wife

Jessica at our house while she took a few moments to enjoy the annual play.

"I remember when it was us in this very play," I said. "You always got to play Mary because you could sit perfectly still for the longest of anyone, and Tommy Guntherman used to be Joseph. Missy Longstrom was the narrator and Becky Smith the angel."

"How do you remember all that?" Levi asked.

"I have an excellent memory. You usually played the donkey and I was the cow. Was there even a cow in the Nativity story?"

Ellie smiled. "You played the cow because all you had to do was stand in the field and try to keep it zipped while the rest of us said our lines."

I glanced at Zak, who was sitting on my left. He was chatting with my father, who was on his left. I'd always enjoyed coming to the Nativity play the church put on every year, but now, with my sweet and cuddly daughter on my lap and my wide-eyed sister in the performance, it was even more special.

"Well, Catherine isn't going to be a cow. She's going to be the angel, or maybe the narrator. I suppose I can deal with her being a lamb when she's very little. But not a cow. Never a cow."

"The cow is cute," Ellie countered.

"Not when you get stuck in that costume for five years in a row."

"Shh, they're starting," Mom said from her seat next to Dad.

I tightened my arms slightly around Catherine and turned my attention to the stage. Harper didn't have any lines, and really all she did was sit, but dang if she wasn't the cutest lamb I'd ever seen.

Afterward, we all headed to our house for tacos, margaritas, and time with family and friends. We put everyone under five down for a nap, and the adults gathered in the living room while the teens hung out in the den.

"Sheriff Salinger is on the phone for you," Dad called from the kitchen, where he was helping Zak prepare the meal. "He said he tried your cell, but you didn't answer."

"I turned the ringer off during the play and must have forgotten to turn it back on. I'll take it in Zak's office," I said.

"Hey, Salinger, what's up?" I asked when I'd sat down at Zak's desk and answered the extension.

"I don't want to interrupt your Sunday, but you did ask me to call if I had news."

"I did. Do you have news?"

"I spoke to the bartender again. He confirmed there was a back room just behind the bar, and that the waiter mixed the whiskey sours he carried around on a counter in there. So that's where the tainted drink Zarek ingested came from, and the bartender saw several other people going in and out of that room too."

I glanced out the window, where the outdoor lights had just switched on. "Like who?"

"Zarek, for one. Earlier, before he set up camp with the senator. Olivia was in and out, as was Carson, although he said Carson mostly stayed out of the room where the guests were."

"Anyone else?"

"That's all he remembered."

"Well, I doubt Zarek poisoned himself, and with the way Olivia's been acting, I sort of doubt she did it. I think it's possible someone paid the waiter to add the toxin to a drink, but the strongest suspect in my mind is still Carson. Have you spoken to him again?"

"I have. He still maintains that while he argued with Zarek earlier in the day and decided to stay well in the background at the cocktail party, he didn't kill him. I don't know if I believe him, but I have no real evidence to suggest that he's lying, so I have no reason to arrest him. I'll keep digging. What we need is the smoking gun."

"The smoking gun?" I asked.

"The vial that held the toxin. If we can find that, I'm hoping we can lift a print from it. I have a team going through Zarek's house and trash again, although I doubt we'll find anything. The killer most likely took it with them when they left."

"It would have been stupid to leave it behind. Have you identified the woman at the bar?"

"Not yet, but I'm still working on it."

"If Carson is guilty, what do you need to make an arrest?"

"Physical evidence would be best. Something like fingerprints on the vial."

"What about fingerprints on the glass Zarek drank from?"

"We already checked that. The only prints were Zarek's and an unmatched set we suspect are the waiter's."

"If you have the prints can't you make an ID?"

"Unmatched basically means they aren't in our system."

"Drat. Okay, if you can't find prints what else could work?"

"A reliable eyewitness statement. If there was a reliable eyewitness, I'd think they would have come through by now, though."

"Without physical evidence or a reliable eyewitness are we dead in the water?"

"Probably, unless someone decides to confess."

I leaned back in Zak's chair. "Then it sounds like we need a confession."

Chapter 14

Monday, December 24

I woke on Christmas Eve to gently falling snow, a happy and smiling baby, three teenagers who were overly excited and therefore bouncing off the walls, and a wonderful husband I loved with my entire heart and soul. I also woke with the realization of who'd killed Zarek. The question was, what would I do with that piece of insight? Should I simply tuck the knowledge in the back of my mind to be dealt with at a later time and enjoy what was intended to be a special family holiday? Or should I take my realization and use it to close this complex and confusing case? Deciding to embrace the team marriage, I consulted Zak, asking for his advice.

"What do you think?" I asked after explaining my entire theory in explicit detail.

"I think you might really be on to something."

"So what do I do? Do I deal with this today or do I wait?"

"I think you call Salinger and then let him deal with it. It is, after all, his job."

I raised a shoulder. "Perhaps. But Salinger said short of physical evidence or a reliable eyewitness, he'd need a confession. I think I have a much better chance than he does of getting that confession."

Zak groaned.

"I won't be in any danger."

"I know."

"And I should be home in three hours, four max."

"I know."

"And," I wrapped my arms around Zak's waist, "once I get home it will be over, and we won't have to speak about it or deal with it ever again. We can have a good old-fashioned family Christmas without Zarek's murder hanging over our heads."

Zak pulled me to his chest and hugged me tight. "Call Salinger. If he agrees with your theory and wants you in on the interview, I'm fine with it."

******

"I wondered who'd come to visit on Christmas Eve." Olivia greeted me from across the metal table in the visitor room at the Bryton Lake jail. "Did you bring cookies?"

I leaned forward slightly. "I brought questions."

Olivia blew out a breath. "Figures. Are you finally ready to believe me when I tell you it was that lowlife Carson Amundson who killed Zarek?"

"Perhaps."

"Good, because there's nothing I'd like better than to see him fry for what he did."

I lowered my voice a bit, digging deep for a tone of sympathy. "I guess you must feel very betrayed by Carson after everything you did for him."

"Betrayed is much too mild a word."

I softened the expression in my eyes. "Yes, I suppose it is. I've given it some thought, and I've realized you were just trying to help him. You loved him and you wanted to show him how much you did by helping him realize his dreams."

Olivia's eyes teared up. "Exactly."

"But despite your sacrifice, Carson rejected you."

Olivia snickered. "After everything I did for that toad, after giving up everything so we could work together to build his dream, the jerk had the nerve to tell me that we didn't have a future together. That there was someone else. That he'd had someone else in mind when he spoke of building a future with his one true love." Olivia looked at me with eyes filled with rage. "Trust me when I say if the man burns for all eternity, it will be too kind an end for that soulless demon."

"I want to help you put Carson away," I said with as much sincerity as I could muster. "I want to help you make certain he does burn. But first I need to understand what happened. I need to know so I can make sure Carson pays for his crime."

Olivia narrowed her gaze. I looked into her eyes but didn't see an ounce of sanity. I wondered if there was anything left of the woman she'd once been.

"Carson used you," I added. "He used you to do what needed to be done and then tossed you away like yesterday's newspaper."

"Damn right he used me. We both knew Zarek and his ridiculous idea to build this überexclusive resort was never going to fly. Carson worked hard on the project. He devoted a lot of his time and money to it, but Zarek was going to ruin everything with his rigidity. Carson and I talked about the fact that if Zarek wasn't in the picture, the senator would probably help make the resort a reality. We talked about how grand it would be to own something so magnificent. We talked about dreams and the realization of them. We talked about the future. We agreed the dream would never happen with Zarek around. I knew he needed to be eliminated, but Carson was such a wimp. He'd never do it, so I took matters into my own hands."

"You added the poison to Zarek's drink."

Olivia's face fell. She looked genuinely grieved. "I thought he'd just go to sleep. I didn't know it would be such a painful end. Or such a fast one. I figured I'd give him the toxin and he'd die later that night, in his sleep. I figured everyone would just think he'd drunk too much at the party."

"But that wasn't how things worked out."

Olivia shook her head. "No. The poison kicked in so fast. It was awful. I didn't know what to do. Not only was Zarek dead but Carson was upset. After the fight they'd had that day, I didn't think he'd care that Zarek was dead. When I saw how sad and angry he was, I knew I couldn't tell him what I'd done, so I pretended to be sad too. I thought Carson would want to comfort me, but instead he sought comfort in the arms of some skank he met while working with the senator. After everything I'd done for him, he was going to build the resort with her. She was the one who was his one true love."

"So you tried to get him arrested for killing Zarek. You wanted him to suffer the way you were suffering."

"Of course I did. And when the useless sheriff wouldn't arrest him, I tried to take care of him the way I'd taken care of Zarek. All that got me was a new residence and this disgusting orange jumpsuit."

I turned my head and glanced behind me. Salinger came in with a prison guard.

"So that's it?" Olivia screamed. "I thought you were going to help me. Please at least tell me you're going to make sure Carson burns for what he did to me."

"I'm sure he's suffering," I assured her as the guard led her back to her cell.

I turned to Salinger. "Is that enough?"

He nodded. "More than enough. She's obviously mentally unstable. Maybe we can use this confession to get her the help she needs."

I certainly hoped so. She'd killed one man and had tried to kill another, but I still hated to see anyone in so much pain.

Chapter 15

Tuesday, December 25

"I'll get her," Zak said, in response to Catherine banging on the wall that separated our bedroom from the nursery.

I looked at the clock. It was just four fifteen in the morning. "It seems someone is excited about Santa."

Zak groaned.

"I'll get her," I offered. "Why don't you turn on the fire and the tree lights? I'll rock her and see if I can't get her back to sleep."

"I think all the excitement that's been going on this week has her off her sleeping schedule," Zak said as he pulled on his robe and padded across the room.

"Ma," Catherine screamed at the top of her lungs.

"I'm coming," I called back as I headed to the nursery. "You do know it's still dark?" I asked when I stood beside her.

"Up." Catherine reached her hands into the air. She sure did look cute in her night-before-Christmas footie pajamas.

I picked Catherine up and snugged her to my chest. "Let's change you and then we can go rock."

"Lele." She pointed to Charlie, who had been sleeping at the foot of our bed but had wandered into the room behind me.

"Yes, Charlie can rock with us." I smoothed Catherine's brown curls away from her face, then kissed her on the cheek. After laying her on the dressing table, I handed her a stuffed toy to hold, changed her diaper, and made sure her jammies were dry. Then I carried her into the main part of the suite where Zak was waiting with a dancing fire, a colorful Christmas tree, and holiday tunes playing softly.

"Da." Catherine reached for Zak.

"Hey there, princess," Zak said, taking his daughter. "Are you too excited to sleep?"

Catherine just giggled.

Zak sat down in the rocking chair. I tucked a warm blanket around Catherine and Zak started to rock. I sat down on the sofa and pulled a comforter over me. Charlie climbed into my lap and I caressed my first baby while Zak rocked his.

"You know, the older kids will be up by the time we get Catherine to sleep," I said as I ran my fingers through Charlie's soft fur.

"I know. But it's Christmas and kids are supposed to get up early on Christmas morning."

"I guess we need to get the hams and turkeys in the oven anyway." I yawned.

"What time is everyone coming over?"

"Mom and Dad and Grandpa and Hazel are coming to have breakfast and open presents at around nine, although if I know my parents, they'll be here earlier. The rest of our guests will be here around eleven so we can have the stocking exchange. I plan to eat between one and two. Did you get all the stockings stuffed before you came up to bed last night?"

"I did. One for every boy and girl from baby Alya to your grandpa."

"It's nice you took the time to buy special trinkets for everyone."

Zak smiled. "It was fun. Hazel was a little tricky, and I don't know Shawna well enough to be sure what she'd like, but hopefully everyone will have fun digging down to the bottom of their stockings and uncovering all the small objects." Zak looked down at the baby in his arms. "It looks like she's back to sleep."

"We have to get up in a couple of hours anyway and we're already awake, and it's so cozy in here, maybe we should exchange our stockings now."

"Before the others wake up?"

I plucked Catherine out of Zak's arms and carried her into the nursery. He followed. "I didn't want to hang your stocking downstairs because you were the one doing the stuffing, so I kept it up here. I could take it down, but some things are sort of personal in nature."

Zak pulled me into his arms after I'd tucked Catherine in. "Personal? How personal are we talking?"

I rose on tiptoe and kissed Zak's neck. "Very personal."

Up Next From Kathi Daley

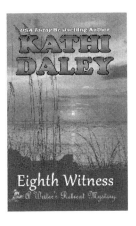

The gang from the Gull Island Writers Retreat take on the case of a man who is currently doing time for the murder of a woman he swears he did not kill. After speaking to the man Alex determines that he is most likely telling the truth so he enlists the help of the gang to prove it.

Abby finds a bundle of letters which had been written in 1954 in the wall of the library after Lonnie tears it down as part of the remodel. Intrigued by the secret revealed in the letters, Abby and Georgia set out to find the rest of the story. Meanwhile, Chief Colt Wilder uncovers a new clue relating to the death of a local girl the previous summer. In spite of her vow to focus her time on her writing, Abby finds herself pulled into the tangled web of half truths that may tell a different story than was first believed true.

Recipes

Snowball Cookies

Pilgrim Pie

Pumpkin Snickerdoodles

Triple Chip Cookie Bars

Snowball Cookies

Mix thoroughly:
2 cups softened butter
1 cup powdered sugar
2 tsp. vanilla

Stir in:
4½ cups flour
1 tsp. salt

Add:
2 cups chopped walnuts

Refrigerate at least 1 hour.

Roll into 1-inch balls and place on ungreased baking sheet. Bake at 400 degrees until set but not brown. While still warm, roll in powdered sugar. Let cool and roll in powdered sugar a second time.

Pilgrim Pie

2 eggs
1 cup brown sugar
1 cup dark corn syrup
1 tsp. vanilla
2 tbs. butter, melted
⅛ tsp. salt
½ cup grated coconut
½ cup rolled oats
½ cup pecans
1 premade pie shell

Beat eggs. Blend in sugar, corn syrup, vanilla, butter, and salt. Stir in coconut, oats, and pecans.

Pour into pie shell.

Bake at 400 degrees for 15 minutes. Reduce oven to 350 degrees and bake for 30 minutes.

Check with knife to see if pie is set. If not, bake until set.

Pumpkin Snickerdoodles

Ingredients:
1 cup butter at room temperature
1 cup granulated sugar
½ cup light brown sugar
¾ cup canned pumpkin
1 large egg
2 tsp. vanilla extract
3¾ cups flour
1½ tsp. baking powder
½ tsp. salt
½ tsp. ground cinnamon
¼ tsp. ground nutmeg

For the coating:
½ cup sugar
1 tsp. cinnamon
½ tsp. ground ginger
Dash of allspice

Whip together butter and sugars until creamy. Add pumpkin, egg, and vanilla. Mix well. Add dry ingredients and mix well.

Refrigerate for at least 1 hour.

In a separate bowl, mix the sugar and spices for the coating. Roll chilled dough into 1-inch balls. Roll in coating.

Bake on ungreased cookie sheet at 400 degrees until lightly brown (around 12 minutes).

Triple Chip Cookie Bars

Graham cracker crust:
3 cups graham cracker crumbs
¾ cup melted margarine
½ cup sugar

Combine and press into 9 x 13 baking pan.

Middle layer:
½ cup chocolate chips
½ cup butterscotch chips
1 can sweetened condensed milk (14 oz.)
1 tsp. vanilla

Microwave for 1 minute; stir, microwave 30 seconds more. Pour over crust.

Topping:
Remainder of large bag of chocolate chips (approx. 11 oz.)
Remainder of large bag of butterscotch chips (approx. 11 oz.)
1 cup white chocolate chips
1½ cups salted peanuts

Pour evenly over crust. Bake at 350 degrees for 25 minutes.

Books by Kathi Daley
Come for the murder, stay for the romance

Zoe Donovan Cozy Mystery:
Halloween Hijinks
The Trouble With Turkeys
Christmas Crazy
Cupid's Curse
Big Bunny Bump-off
Beach Blanket Barbie
Maui Madness
Derby Divas
Haunted Hamlet
Turkeys, Tuxes, and Tabbies
Christmas Cozy
Alaskan Alliance
Matrimony Meltdown
Soul Surrender
Heavenly Honeymoon
Hopscotch Homicide
Ghostly Graveyard
Santa Sleuth
Shamrock Shenanigans
Kitten Kaboodle
Costume Catastrophe
Candy Cane Caper
Holiday Hangover
Easter Escapade
Camp Carter
Trick or Treason
Reindeer Roundup
Hippity Hoppity Homicide

Firework Fiasco
Henderson House
Holiday Hostage
Lunacy Lake – *Summer 2019*

Zimmerman Academy The New Normal
Zimmerman Academy New Beginnings
Ashton Falls Cozy Cookbook

Tj Jensen Paradise Lake Mysteries by Henery Press:

Pumpkins in Paradise
Snowmen in Paradise
Bikinis in Paradise
Christmas in Paradise
Puppies in Paradise
Halloween in Paradise
Treasure in Paradise
Fireworks in Paradise
Beaches in Paradise
Thanksgiving in Paradise – *Fall 2019*

Whales and Tails Cozy Mystery:

Romeow and Juliet
The Mad Catter
Grimm's Furry Tail
Much Ado About Felines
Legend of Tabby Hollow
Cat of Christmas Past
A Tale of Two Tabbies
The Great Catsby
Count Catula
The Cat of Christmas Present

A Winter's Tail
The Taming of the Tabby
Frankencat
The Cat of Christmas Future
Farewell to Felines
A Whisker in Time
The Catsgiving Feast
A Whale of a Tail – *Spring 2019*

Writers' Retreat Southern Seashore Mystery:
First Case
Second Look
Third Strike
Fourth Victim
Fifth Night
Sixth Cabin
Seventh Chapter
Eighth Witness – *January 2019*

Rescue Alaska Paranormal Mystery:

Finding Justice
Finding Answers
Finding Courage
Finding Christmas
Finding Motive – *Spring 2019*

A Tess and Tilly Mystery:

The Christmas Letter
The Valentine Mystery
The Mother's Day Mishap
The Halloween House
The Thanksgiving Trip
The Saint Paddy's Promise – *March 2019*

The Inn at Holiday Bay:

Boxes in the Basement
Letters in the Library – *February 2019*
Message in the Mantle – *Spring 2019*

Family Ties:

The Hathaway Sisters
Harper – *Spring 2019*
Harlow – *Summer 2019*
Haven – *Fall 2019*
Haley – *Winter 2019*

Haunting by the Sea:

Homecoming by the Sea
Secrets by the Sea
Missing by the Sea

Deception by the Sea – *Spring 2019*
Betrayal by the Sea – *Summer 2019*
Christmas by the Sea – *Fall 2019*

Sand and Sea Hawaiian Mystery:
Murder at Dolphin Bay
Murder at Sunrise Beach
Murder at the Witching Hour
Murder at Christmas
Murder at Turtle Cove
Murder at Water's Edge
Murder at Midnight

Seacliff High Mystery:
The Secret
The Curse
The Relic
The Conspiracy
The Grudge
The Shadow
The Haunting

Road to Christmas Romance:
Road to Christmas Past

USA Today best-selling author Kathi Daley lives in beautiful Lake Tahoe with her husband Ken. When she isn't writing, she likes spending time hiking the miles of desolate trails surrounding her home. She has authored more than seventy-five books in eight series, including Zoe Donovan Cozy Mysteries, Whales and Tails Island Mysteries, Sand and Sea Hawaiian Mysteries, Tj Jensen Paradise Lake Series, Writers' Retreat Southern Seashore Mysteries, Rescue Alaska Paranormal Mysteries, and Seacliff High Teen Mysteries. Find out more about her books at **www.kathidaley.com**

Stay up-to-date:

Newsletter, *The Daley Weekly*
http://eepurl.com/NRPDf
Webpage – **www.kathidaley.com**
Facebook at Kathi Daley Books –
www.facebook.com/kathidaleybooks
Kathi Daley Books Group Page –
**https://www.facebook.com/groups/5695788231468
50/**
E-mail – **kathidaley@kathidaley.com**
Twitter at Kathi Daley@kathidaley –
https://twitter.com/kathidaley
Amazon Author Page –
https://www.amazon.com/author/kathidaley
BookBub –
https://www.bookbub.com/authors/kathi-daley

18042159R00109

Made in the USA
San Bernardino, CA
19 December 2018